★ "If it ain't broke, don't fix it, and Gidwitz deploys his successful formula of bloody happenings and narratorial intrusion in his third and final installment of unexpurgated fairy tales. . . . Underneath the gore, the wit, and the trips to Hell and back, this book makes it clearer than ever that Gidwitz truly cares about the kids he writes for."
—*PUBLISHERS WEEKLY*, starred review

"Entertaining story-mongering, with traditional and original tropes artfully intertwined."
—*KIRKUS*

"As innovative as they are traditional, the stories maintain clear connections with traditional Grimm tales while creatively connecting to the narrative, and all the while keeping the proceedings undeniably grisly and lurid. . . . Readers will rejoice."
—*SCHOOL LIBRARY JOURNAL*

HONORS & ACCOLADES FOR THE GRIMM SERIES

New York Times bestseller

TODAY Show Al's Book Club for Kids pick

E. B. White Read Aloud Award Honor Book

ALA Notable Book

New York Times Book Review Editors' Choice selection

Kirkus Best Book of the Year

Publishers Weekly Best Book of the Year

School Library Journal Best Book of the Year

Bank Street College of Education Best Book of the Year

ALSO BY
ADAM GIDWITZ

A COMPANION TO
A TALE DARK &
GRIMM

THE GRIMM CONCLUSION

ADAM GIDWITZ

DUTTON CHILDREN'S BOOKS

DUTTON CHILDREN'S BOOKS
An imprint of Penguin Random House LLC, New York

First published in the United States of America by Dutton Children's Books,
an imprint of Penguin Random House LLC, 2013
This paperback edition published 2021

Text copyright © 2013 by Adam Gidwitz
Illustrations copyright © 2013 by Hugh D'Andrade
Excerpt from *A Tale Dark & Grimm* text copyright © 2010 by Adam Gidwitz
Excerpt from *A Tale Dark & Grimm* illustrations copyright © 2010 by Hugh D'Andrade

Visit us online at penguinrandomhouse.com.

THE LIBRARY OF CONGRESS HAS CATALOGED THE DUTTON CHILDREN'S BOOKS EDITION AS FOLLOWS:
The Grimm conclusion / Adam Gidwitz.—First edition.
pages cm
Companion to: A tale dark & Grimm and In a glass Grimmly
Summary: "Sister and brother Jorinda and Joringel fight to keep their promise to stay together throughout
a series of gruesome, twisted Grimm-inspired short stories"
—Provided by the publisher.
ISBN 978-0-525-42615-8 (hardcover)
[1. Fairy tales. 2. Characters in literature—Fiction. 3. Brothers and sisters—Fiction.
4. Adventure and adventurers—Fiction. 5. Humorous stories.]
I. Grimm, Jacob, 1785–1863. II. Grimm, Wilhelm, 1786–1859. III. Title.
PZ8.G36Gr 2013 [Fic]—dc23 2013021686

ISBN 9780142427361

Edited by Julie Strauss-Gabel
Creative Direction by Deborah Kaplan
Designed by Kristin Smith and Irene Vandervoort

Printed in the United States of America

10

For every kid I've ever told a story to.

Contents

Once upon a time, fairy tales were grim.

The Merriam-Webster Dictionary defines the word *grim* as "ghastly, repellent, or sinister in character." Their example of how to use the word is this: "a *grim* tale." (Really! It says that!)

Once upon a time, fairy tales were Grimm, too. That is, they were collected by the brothers Jacob and Wilhelm Grimm.

You know the tales of the Brothers Grimm.

For example, raise your hand if you've ever heard of a story called "Little Red Riding Hood."

You haven't?

Oh, you have. Then why aren't you raising your hand? Go ahead and raise it. I don't care how stupid you look, sitting in the corner of the library by yourself, or on the school bus, or in bed at night, raising your hand for no apparent reason. How else am I supposed to know whether you've read "Little Red Riding Hood"?

Raise it.

Thank you.

Okay, raise your hand if you've heard of "Hansel and Gretel."

Do it.

Thanks.

Raise your hand if you've heard of "Rumpelstiltskin." (I assume you're raising your hand.)

"Sleeping Beauty." (Your hand's still up, right?)

"Snow White." (Of course you have.)

"Cinderella." (Your hand *better* still be in the air.)

But now you're thinking: *Wait a minute. You said fairy tales used to be grim—i.e., ghastly, repellent, sinister. These stories aren't ghastly, repellent, or sinister at all. They are cute, and sweet, and* boring.

And, I must admit, these days you are correct. The versions of these stories that most people tell are indeed cute and sweet and incredibly, mind-numbingly, want-to-hit-yourself-in-the-head-with-a-sledgehammer-ingly boring.

But the original fairy tales were not.

Take "Rumpelstiltskin," for example. You may know "Rumpelstiltskin" as a funny little tale about a funny little man with a funny not-all-that-little name.

But do you remember what happens at the end of that funny little story? The girl guesses his name, right? And he gets very angry. And do you remember what happens then?

No?

Well, in some versions of the story, Rumpelstiltskin stamps his foot and flies out the window.

Which makes no sense. Who has ever stamped their foot and suddenly gone flying out of a window? Impossible.

In other versions of the story, he stamps his foot and shatters into a thousand pieces.

This is even more ridiculous than him flying out of a window. People don't shatter. People are fleshy and bloody and gooey. *Shatter* is not something that people do.

So what actually happens when the girl guesses Rumpelstiltskin's name? In the real, Grimm version of the story?

Well, he stamps his foot so hard that it gets buried three feet in the ground. Then he grabs his other leg, and he pulls up on it with such force that he *rips himself in half.*

Which, it must be admitted, is indeed ghastly, repellent, sinister—and *awesome*.

The story I am about to tell you is like that, too.

It is Grimm. And grim.

In fact, it is the grimmest, Grimmest tale that I have ever heard.

And I am sharing it with you.

Yeah. You're welcome.

Jorinda
and Joringel

Once upon a time, in the days when fairy tales really happened, there lived a man and his wife. They were a happy couple, for they had everything their hearts desired. They had a little house, a little garden, and in the center of that garden, they had a pretty little juniper tree.

Yes, they had everything their hearts desired. Everything, that is, except a child. More than anything else—more than their house, their garden, their tree—this couple wanted a child. But they did not have one.

One winter's day, the wife stood in the garden beneath the juniper tree—which is a handsome pine with needles so dark they are almost blue and little red berries that look like drops of blood.

She was peeling an apple with a knife when her hand slipped, and she cut herself. A drop of her blood fell to the snowy ground. She saw the drop of blood on the snow, and she thought, "Oh, how I wish I had a child, as red as blood and as white as snow."

Hold on. I have to interrupt.

You think you know this story. You think it's "Snow White."

You think wrong.

If I wanted to be educational, I would explain that fairy tales often share "motifs" with one another—images and phrases that crop up again and again, even in tales from different countries and cultures. Which is a little bit interesting.

I do not, though, have any desire to be educational.

No. I just want to tell you this completely messed-up story.

Well, a month went by, and the snow with it. Two months, and the world was green. Three months, and flowers came out of the ground. Four months, and the trees of the forest pressed hard upon one another and the green branches all mingled together. The fifth month passed, and the wife stood under the juniper tree as its blossoms fell to the earth. When the sixth month was

ADAM GIDWITZ

gone, the berries had grown big and firm, and the woman became very still. After the seventh month, she snatched at the juniper berries and ate so greedily she grew sad and sickened. When the eighth month had passed, she called her husband and wept and said, "If I die, bury me under the juniper tree." With that she took comfort and was happy until the ninth month. Then she bore twins: a little boy with dark hair, dark eyes, and lips as red as blood; and a little girl with dark hair and green eyes and cheeks as white as snow.

She brought them to her husband. This man took one look at his two beautiful children, and he was so happy that he died.

WHAT? He was so happy that he *died*?

Yup.

That sort of thing used to happen all the time. It was just . . . "Oh, I'm so happy! I'm so happy! I'm so ha-a-a-ack-ack-ack . . ."

Dead.

On the infants' very first night in this world, their mother sat by the fire and wept with joy for her living children and with grief for her dead husband. The infants, off in their crib, wondered where their mother was, and why she was not holding them, and where that distant crying sound was coming from. At last, because a baby needs to be held, the infant girl reached out her tiny hand, and the infant boy reached out his, and they held on to one another.

Now, this mother was a very learned woman. She was known far and wide for her collection of old books and her mastery of dead languages. But no amount of learning or knowledge had prepared her to raise two children on her own. She had no books for that—and what she did read about children in her ancient books had very little to do with these two delicate, squirming, crying creatures.

She was afraid. She feared that she would raise them badly. So she pretty much left them alone. She would feed them and clothe them and then she would retire to her study and pore over her ancient books in dead languages and try not to think too much about the babies who cried for her from the room upstairs.

Well, these babies grew, as babies will. Soon they were scampering around on their own, laughing and running and playing.

Everywhere the little boy went, the little girl went. And everywhere the little girl went, the little boy went. They tended to the house together and played together out of doors and tucked themselves in bed at night and told each other bedtime stories—so their mother wouldn't have to stop her studies. And they rarely called each other by their names, which were strange and German and hard to pronounce. They called each other Little Brother and Little Sister, even though they were just about exactly the same age. They loved each other so dearly that one grew sad when the other was out of sight. The little boy would often say to his sister, "If you won't leave me, I won't leave you." To which the little girl would always reply, "I will never, ever leave you."

Now, even though the children called one another Little Brother and Little Sister, I can't manage to tell their entire story without using their names. I did try, but it gets very confusing. For example, if I want to let you know that one of them looked little, I can't say, "The enormous, murderous ogre peered down at little Little Sister." That would sound weird.

Since I'm going to need to use their names, you're going to have to learn to pronounce them. Even if the children, generally, didn't bother.

The little girl's name was Jorinda. You pronounce that YOUR-INDA.

The little boy's name was Joringel. You pronounce that: YOUR-INGLE.

Yes, German is weird.

As the years went by, the mother became more and more worried about her children. She worried that she neglected them, and she worried that they had no one who knew how to guide their growth properly.

So she decided to marry again. She consulted all the ancient books that she owned, considered all the single men in the village, and decided on her husband.

The man she chose was neither handsome nor very kind, but he was a good cook, and the mother had read that growing children need good, hearty food to help them grow.

Also, he had two beautiful daughters, just a little bit older than Jorinda and Joringel. So the man knew how to raise children. That, the mother decided, was good, too.

And everything was good. For a few days.

Jorinda (that's the girl) and Joringel (that's the boy) always cleaned the house and took care of all the chores, so their mother did not have to interrupt her important studies. Well, one day, they asked their new stepsisters if they wanted to help clean the house.

The girls flipped their long, beautiful hair and laughed. "Why would we *want* to help?"

"You look like you're doing a fine job on your own!"

And they walked away giggling.

So Jorinda and Joringel went into the kitchen where their stepfather was cooking and asked if they could have some help with the laundry, now that there was twice as much of it to do. He brandished a wooden spoon and chased them away.

Soon, Jorinda and Joringel began to realize that their new family members did not like them very much. In fact, the stepsisters loathed Jorinda and teased her cruelly. And the stepfather hated Joringel with a passion as hot as the hottest coal. I don't know why. He just did.

One day, Jorinda and Joringel found themselves standing outside their mother's study.

The little boy sniffled hard. "I wish Mama would come out."

"Shh," said Jorinda. "Don't disturb her."

Joringel's jaw was moving sideways, back and forth. This either meant he was thinking about something or he was going to cry. Jorinda was nervous about both possibilities.

"I'm going to knock," said Joringel.

"Don't!" Jorinda hissed. But before she could stop him, he had rapped three times on the door of their mother's study.

Behind the door, they could hear a chair being pushed back and pages being shuffled. "Coming!" a voice called.

Jorinda tried to pull her brother away, but Joringel stood firm.

The door opened, and their mother appeared. Her long hair was held up in a messy bun behind her head, and she was blinking, as if she weren't used to looking at anything that wasn't words on a page. When she saw the children, she smiled sadly and knelt before them.

"Yes, my dears?" she asked.

Suddenly, Joringel didn't know what to say. He looked at the floor.

"Nothing, Mama," Jorinda cut in. "We're sorry to disturb you."

But her mother said, "You're not disturbing me. What is it?"

Joringel raised his head. His eyes were brimming with tears.

The mother took her children by their small hands and led them into her study.

The walls were lined with ancient volumes, huge books bound with leather and nails. It smelled musty in there, but the sunlight slanted warm and bright through the small window. Jorinda and Joringel felt like they were entering a secret temple. Neither breathed.

The mother sat down by her desk and, holding her children's hands, looked into their eyes. "What's bothering you?" she asked.

Joringel said, "I wish we had our real father with us."

His mother nodded. "So do I. Every day. Every night, when I try to sleep, the pain is like a stone under my mattress. But do you know what to do when there's a stone under your mattress that you just can't get rid of?"

"What?"

"Get another mattress, and another, and another. Bury the stone under mattresses, until you don't feel it anymore."

Joringel squinted. "You sleep with lots of mattresses on your bed, Mama?"

His mother smiled. "It's a metaphor."

Joringel didn't know what a metaphor was. Neither did Jorinda, but she wasn't about to let the longest conversation they had had with their mother in years end yet. So she said, "I hate our stepsisters. They're selfish, and they're mean."

Her mother pressed her lips together. Then she said, "Anger is a weed, Jorinda. It grows up through the soil, choking every other plant. You must stamp it out. Don't let it enter your garden. Stamp out your anger until it never comes back."

Both children held their faces tight. Jorinda was trying to

stamp out her anger. Joringel was trying to smother his pain. Suddenly, a single tear choked its way out of Joringel's eye. His mother reached out her finger and caught it. She wiped it on her shirt. "And never cry," she said. "Choke back your tears. Tears are waves on the ocean of sadness. You will drown in them if you're not careful. Believe me. I know."

Then Jorinda and Joringel's mother turned back to the ancient books on her desk. She clenched her jaw and exhaled through her nose, like she was steeling herself against something. She began to read.

Jorinda took her brother by the arm and led him away.

Excuse me. I have a question.

What do you think of the advice that Jorinda and Joringel's mother just gave them?

Is it good to stamp out your anger? To choke back your tears? To smother your pain? Is that how you find peace?

I'm just wondering. 'Cause I'd like to know.

Also, you're probably thinking, *Hey! You promised to tell us a grim and messed-up story. This story isn't messed up. It's all emotional and stuff!*

Yeah, I'm sorry about that.

But we have now arrived at the part of the tale that might fairly be described as ghastly, repellent, and sinister.

In other words, the part you've been waiting for.

You have been warned.

It was morning, and Jorinda and Joringel's stepfather was in the kitchen with his daughters, taking big red apples from a marketing basket and putting them in a large chest with a big heavy lid and a sharp brass lock, when Jorinda and Joringel came in.

Jorinda, seeing the lovely apples, said, "Stepfather, may I have an apple?"

The man said, "Of course, my dear." And he handed the little girl an apple. The stepsisters scowled.

And then Joringel said, "Stepfather, may I have an apple, too?"

"NO!" the man bellowed. And he snatched the apple back from Jorinda, threw it into the chest, and slammed the heavy lid shut.

The stepsisters laughed loudly.

A few minutes later, Jorinda was outside weeding the garden while Joringel mopped the floors in the living room. The stepfather approached the little boy. The man's voice was gentle when he said, "I'm sorry I snapped at you. Would you like an apple now?"

Joringel nodded.

His stepfather smiled. "Then follow me."

So Joringel followed his stepfather past his mother's study and into the kitchen. The stepsisters were nowhere to be seen. The man walked over to the great chest of apples. He unlatched the sharp brass lock and lifted the heavy lid with a creak of hinges. "There," he said to the little boy. "Choose any apple you want."

Joringel bent down and leaned his head over the apples. They smelled fresh and rich, and their yellow skin was dappled with rose and—

BANG!

The stepfather slammed the lid of the chest down.

Right on the back of Joringel's neck.

And the little boy's head fell off into the apples.

For a moment, there was no sound in the kitchen at all, and the only movement was the dust dancing in the slants of light from the window. The stepfather stood stock-still over the chest. The boy's small, headless body lay on the floor. Blood pooled under his severed neck. His head, of course, was in the chest of apples.

And then his stepfather said, "Oh no! His mother will be furious with me!"

ADAM GIDWITZ

Wait, he just *killed* the kid, and he's worried his wife will be *ticked off*?

You think?

The stepfather gathered up the little boy's body and carried it to a chair that sat near the front of the house. Then he went to the kitchen, opened the chest, retrieved Joringel's head, and took it over to his body. He placed the head on the severed neck, and then tied it on with a white handkerchief. Finally, he put a fine red apple in the little boy's hand.

Joringel sat in the chair, eyes wide and staring, facing the front door.

The stepfather surveyed his handiwork, nodded once, and went back to the kitchen to clean up.

Is everyone okay out there?

I will remind you that, just because this is a fairy tale, that does *not* mean that it is appropriate for little children. Little children should not be hearing stories about decapitation and infanticide. In fact, anyone who's young enough not to know the words *decapitation* and *infanticide* should probably put this book down right now.

Okay? Did you do it?

No, I didn't think you would.

A little while later, Jorinda went looking for her brother. She found him sitting in the chair by the front door, his head tilting slightly off to one side, his eyes wide, an apple in his hand, and a handkerchief around his neck. The handkerchief was red.

"Little Brother, Little Brother! What a lovely apple you have!" she exclaimed. "Will you share it with me?"

But her brother just stared at her, deathly still.

Jorinda began to feel frightened. She went into the kitchen to find her stepfather scrubbing the floor. "Father, Father!" she said. "I think there's something the matter with Little Brother! His eyes are wide and staring, his face is pale, and when I asked him to share his apple with me, he didn't say anything at all!"

The stepfather shook his head. "Oh, he's just being rude. Go back in there and ask him to share it with you again. If he still doesn't reply, slap him in the face."

Oh, yes—he said that.

So the little girl went back into the front room and said, "Brother, Brother, will you share your apple with me?"

And he said . . .

Nothing. Because he was dead.

So the little girl took a deep breath, looked ruefully toward the kitchen, cocked her hand back, and slapped her brother in the face.

And his head fell off.

"OH, MY GOD, I KILLED MY BROTHER!" the little girl screamed.

Her stepfather burst from the kitchen, saw the boy's head lying on the floor, and bellowed, "What have you done, you wicked child?" He glanced at the closed door of the study and hissed, "Your mother will be furious with you!"

Jorinda was hyperventilating.

The man took her by the arms and whispered, "There, there, my dear. Don't cry. Come in the kitchen." And then he added, "I'll help you hide the body."

So the stepfather dragged the little boy's body into the kitchen, and Jorinda carried her beloved brother's head after him. And then the stepfather took out a big knife, and he carved the meat from Joringel's bones.

And he threw it into their largest stew pot.

At this point, I imagine that every adult reading this book aloud has just slammed it shut and said, "Never mind. Forget it. We're done here."

And half the kids are probably screaming for their mothers. And the other half are screaming at the adult to keep reading because this is, well, completely awesome.

Let me say that I agree with all parties involved. Adults, you really should not read any further. Kids who want your moms, you should probably go get them. Kids who think this is awesome, you have never been more right.

What did I tell you about fairy tales? Did I lie?

Once the father was done carving the meat from the boy's bones and putting it into the stew pot, he said, "Now open the icebox."

The icebox was a deep hole, just behind the kitchen, where

ADAM GIDWITZ

perishables were kept. It was cool and damp, and became icy in winter. Hence the name.

Jorinda, still hyperventilating, opened the icebox, and the stepfather lowered the stew pot into it.

"This'll keep for a good long while," he said. And then he turned to the little girl and stuck a thick finger in her face. "If you ever mention this to anyone, you'll be hanged. But first, I'll make you eat this stew."

Finally, the man led his stepdaughter back into the kitchen, where he took the boy's bones, tied them up in a kerchief, and handed them to Jorinda. "Go," he said. "Bury these under the juniper tree."

So Jorinda went into the garden, stood under the juniper tree, and buried her brother's bones.

As she scooped the last handful of black soil onto the makeshift little grave, a tear ran down her cheek, and she thought, You said you'd never leave me.

Okay! I'm sorry!

I know, I know.

This is bad. This is, maybe, the worst thing that you have ever read, in any book, ever.

I am sorry for that.

But let me say this: While I do like messed-up stories, and I do like stories where grim, bloody, horrible things happen, I do *not* like stories with sad endings.

I hate them, in fact.

So lots of grim, bloody, horrible things will keep happening in this book, but everything will turn out okay in the end. I promise you.

Of course, before things get better, they'll probably get worse.

Ready?

Then buckle up, and let's do this thing.

Ashputtle

Before I even *say* "Once upon a time," I've got to tell you something.

"Ashputtle," which is the title of this chapter, is the Grimm brothers' name for "Cinderella."

And now you are worried.

You do not want to hear the story of Cinderella, because you have heard it ten hundred thousand million times, and it makes you want to hit yourself in the head with a sledgehammer.

Good. I'm glad you don't want to hear the story of Cinderella, because I don't want to tell it.

I want to tell you the story of Ashputtle.

"Cinderella" is the name of the cute version of the story,

the one that makes little girls want to dress up like pretty princesses.

That story makes me want to hit myself in the head with a sledgehammer, also.

"Ashputtle" is the name of the horrible, bloody, Grimm, awesome version of the story.

It will *not* make little girls want to dress up like pretty princesses. It will make little girls want to run out of the room screaming for their mommies.

It will make little boys want to do that, too.

So if there are any little girls or little boys in the room, please—for their sakes, and for their mommies' sakes . . .

Do not let them hear this story.

Once upon a time, a little girl named Jorinda knelt under a juniper tree and tried not to weep.

She had, as far as she could tell, killed her brother. She was confused, a bit, by how his head had fallen off with just a slap across the face. She hadn't even slapped him very hard. But his head had fallen off nonetheless. No question about it. And now his bones were buried under the juniper tree, and his flesh sat in a stew pot in the icebox out back.

Jorinda, kneeling beneath the tree, tried to choke back the tears that pressed at her eyes, just as her mother had told her to. But it was not easy.

And then, the little girl felt a tickle on her shoulder. She raised her head. There, sitting just beside her ear, was a little bird. It was as red as blood and as white as snow. It cocked its head left and right as it looked at her. Jorinda smiled. It reminded her of her brother.

"Hello," she said. "What's your name?" It flittered its wings and pecked her twice on the nose, gently. She laughed.

And from that moment on, Jorinda spent every moment of her free time beneath the juniper tree, and the little bird played in the dirt around her feet and chirruped at her and pecked her happily on the nose.

But while Jorinda's friendship with the bird lightened her heart a little bit, her life in the house became worse. Her mother barely seemed to notice that Joringel was gone. She asked about him, absently, one night, and before Jorinda could say a word, her stepfather replied that Joringel had gone off to visit with his uncle in the country. Jorinda's mother tried to remember if Jorinda and Joringel had an uncle living in the country. After a moment, she shrugged her shoulders and went back to her study. Jorinda stared in disbelief.

Jorinda's work around the house became much harder than before. Without her brother to help her, she had twice as many windows to clean, twice as much floor to scrub, twice as much laundry to wash in the cold, cold stream that ran behind their garden. And they began to call her "Ashputtle."

Why, you might ask, did they call her Ashputtle?

Well, you might think it was because her job was to clean the chimney and fireplace, making her all covered with ashes and cinders.

Which is fifty percent correct. That is one reason she was covered in ashes and cinders. But there is another reason, one that is never mentioned in any of the cute, boring, pretty-princess versions of this story.

You see, the other half of the reason that she was covered in ashes and cinders was that her job was to clean the chamber pots. What, you ask, is a chamber pot? A chamber pot is a bowl that is used like a toilet, but doesn't have a hole or water at the bottom. It's just a pot that you go potty in, if you know what I mean. So, you sit on this little pot, and you do your business. Then you leave your business in the pot. Eventually, someone comes around and pours all your business into a bucket. Then they scrub the pot with water and ashes and cinders, until it's as clean as they can make it, and until they're covered in ashes and cinders and . . . well . . . whatever business you left in the pot.

And *that* is why the girl was called Ashputtle.

Once upon a time, everyone who heard the name "Ashputtle"—or "Cinderella," for that matter—knew exactly what it meant.

Toilet Cleaner.

Her name was Toilet Cleaner.

By the way, the next time you see a little girl who's excited for Halloween, and she says, "I want to be Cinderella! I want to be Cinderella!" you'll know that what she's actually saying is, "I want to be Toilet Cleaner! I want to be Toilet Cleaner!"

But don't tell her that, because she'll cry.

So Jorinda, whom the stepsisters and stepfather called Ashputtle, scrubbed the floors and cleaned the windows and the fireplace and the chamber pots. And, late at night, she would go out to the little juniper tree, and the bird would come down and flit back and forth between her feet, and the candle in her mother's study would burn yellow and warm, and Jorinda would try not to cry at the lonely, wreck of a life she now led.

And then, one day, everything changed.

For an invitation arrived.

It was an invitation to a ball. Hosted by the prince of the Kingdom of Grimm. He wanted to marry someone. In order to choose this someone, all the girls of the kingdom were invited to the palace for three nights of dancing and socializing and whatever else you do at a ball. The stepsisters were very excited, of course.

Jorinda, on the other hand, was not excited, because she wasn't allowed to go. Her stepfather made her sew her sisters' dresses and help them prepare and tell them how lovely they looked. And they said nice things to her like, "Oh, it's such a shame you can't come with us!" And then they would look at one another and laugh.

But of course, she will get to go, won't she? Someone gives her a beautiful dress and shoes to wear, right?

Who gives them to her?

Her fairy godmother!

And the fairy godmother is plump and wears purple and has little wings, and goes "Bippity boppity boop!"

Right?

Right?

Wrong.

What really happened was that, on the day of the ball, after the stepsisters had left, Jorinda went out to the juniper tree. She tried not to cry. She tried to choke back her tears. She did not want to drown in the ocean of sadness, whatever that was. But all of the horrible things that had happened crowded in on her. And a tear fell from her lashes into the dirt.

As the tear fell, Jorinda wished she could go to the ball. She wished she could meet the prince. She wished that he would like her. Like her better than her sisters. She wished that he might marry her and take her away from her stepfather and stepsisters, away from this terrible life, away from this house with her brother's empty bed and her mother's closed door. She wished she could be a princess, and sleep on a stack of mattresses a mile high, and never feel this pain—any pain—ever again.

And just as she wished it, a little red berry, as dark and rich and red as blood, fell from the branches of the tree. Little Jorinda picked it up delicately, between her fingers. She pressed it. It burst. Red juice ran down her palm. But suddenly, it was not juice. It was a dress. A long, flowing, beautiful dress exactly as deep and rich and red as blood.

And then, two shoes clunked down out of the tree after it.

What were the shoes made of?

Go ahead and say it . . .

They were made of . . .

Glass!

Right?

Right?

Wrong again!

Gold. The shoes were made of pure gold.

(Fancy, huh?)

Jorinda cried, "Thank you, tree!" She turned toward the house. But just then, the little bird as red as blood and as white as snow landed upon her shoulder. Jorinda looked at it and smiled. It began to sing, and its song sounded almost like words. Like these words:

Before midnight come right back here,
Or else the dress will disappear!

The little girl smiled and thanked the bird and petted it on its small white head. Then she went inside to change.

———

Okay, the next part you know. You know she went to the ball. You know her breath was taken away at the beauty of the palace, and all the important guests, and the fine food, and so on and so forth.

You know she danced with the prince, and that he liked her.

Like, *really* liked her.

Like, *like* liked her.

And you know that they danced all night.

But you also know that, as midnight approached, Jorinda remembered what the bird said—that at midnight the dress would disappear.

Now, I don't know if you've ever been to a ball, with a prince. But in case you ever go, there is one rule you really ought to aware of.

Do not be *naked*.

Not allowed.

Not okay.

So just before midnight, Jorinda broke free from the prince's arms, fled down the steps of the palace, and ran out into the night. And as she ran, the clocks struck twelve, and the dress fell from her shoulders in shreds and tatters.

———

Well, Jorinda went back to the ball the next night. I guess she went to the juniper tree and got another dress or something. I don't know. Not important.

So she danced with the prince the second night, and he really, really liked her. But she had to run away before midnight again, because, as we discussed, *ball* plus *prince* plus *naked* equals *not okay.*

The third night, Jorinda returned to the ball, and again she danced with the prince.

But—and this is an important plot point, so pay attention now—this prince was a *clever* prince.

He knew she was going to run away. And so he told his servants that, while he danced with this mysterious, constantly-running-away girl, they were to smear the steps of the palace with tar—which is the black sticky stuff we use to make roads.

And when midnight came, Jorinda ran out the doors, down the steps, and one of her shoes stuck to a sticky, tarred step. Now, Jorinda kept going (luckily—because of the whole *ball-prince-naked* thing), but her shoe stayed behind. The prince came out of the palace and picked the shoe up and examined it.

And then he exclaimed, "Whoever's foot fits in this golden shoe will be my bride!"

One of his servants leaned over to him. "You think only one girl in the whole kingdom wears a size five?"

And the prince said, "Shut up."

So the prince went from house to house in his kingdom, trying to find the girl whose foot would fit in the golden shoe. But, lo and behold, none did. Some were too wide, some too narrow, some too long, some too short.

Surprising. But totally true.

At last, the prince arrived at Jorinda's house, announcing that whoever's foot fit in the golden shoe would be his bride.

Now, the stepsisters were thrilled. As I said, they were very beautiful—and they knew it. They had beautiful hair, beautiful teeth, beautiful eyes, and tiny, perfect, beautiful feet.

So the elder stepsister flipped her long golden hair and said, "Oh, let me try! Let me try the shoe!" She grabbed the golden shoe from the prince and took it into the kitchen, and her father followed her.

There in the kitchen, the elder stepsister slipped her perfect, delicate little foot into the shoe.

And guess what?

It fit.

Well, almost.

You see, her big toe was just a little bit too big. She couldn't get it all the way in the shoe. She pushed and pushed and pushed, but it just would not go in.

And then her father took out a knife.

The knife was a large cleaver, the kind made for chopping up meat.

He whispered to his daughter, "Just cut off your toe! When you're queen, you won't have to walk anymore!"

So the girl took the cleaver, raised it above her head, and brought it down with all her force on her big toe. Then she shoved her dismembered foot into the shoe, gritted her teeth against the pain, and went back in to see the prince.

Now, I like to picture this part of the story.

This girl wants to marry the prince, right? So she's got to impress him. Which means she ought to smile. But she has just cut off her *toe* and shoved her foot into a *golden shoe*. Which probably hurts *a lot*. Right?

ADAM GIDWITZ

So, if you would, try to grit your teeth in unbearable pain and smile at the same time.

Done it? Okay? Do you look ridiculous?

I thought so.

That is exactly how the stepsister looked.

Anyway, the girl hobbled out of the kitchen, grit her teeth, smiled, spread her arms wide, and cried, "IT FITS!"

And the prince cried out, "MY TRUE BRIDE!" And he lifted her up, carried her outside, put her on his horse, and rode away with her.

Yes. Really.

But he hadn't gone very far when they passed the juniper tree. And up in the juniper tree sat that little bird as red as blood and as white as snow. As the prince and the sister rode by, the little bird called out,

Coo, coo!

There's blood in the shoe!

The foot's too long,

The foot's too wide,

This is not the proper bride!

Well, the prince pulled up his horse and stopped and listened.

Because, when birds *talk*, you should *listen*.

'Cause it's weird.

Well, the prince listened. He turned and looked at the stepsister sitting on the back of his horse. He looked from her long golden hair, past her beautiful face, down her beautiful dress, to the golden shoe.

And indeed, he saw blood burbling up out of it.

He thought about it for a minute. And then he said, "Hey! This isn't the right girl!"

I told you. Clever prince.

So he took the girl home and said, "Do you have any other daughters?" Well, the second sister stepped forward, flipped her long black hair, and said, "Oh, let me try! Let me try the shoe!" So she took the shoe (which I suppose now was filled with blood), and she went to the kitchen, and her father followed her. And she slid her perfect, beautiful little foot into the golden shoe.

And it fit.

Almost.

You see, her heel was just a little bit too big. She pushed and pushed and pushed, but it just would not go in. So her father took out that big old meat cleaver and said, "Cut off a chunk of your heel. When you're queen, you won't have to walk anymore!"

So the stepsister took the meat cleaver and chopped off a chunk of her heel. Then she shoved her foot into the shoe, clenched her teeth against the pain, and went out to see the prince. When she saw him, she gritted her teeth, smiled, spread out her arms, and cried, "IT FITS!"

"MY TRUE BRIDE!" the prince exclaimed. And he picked her up, carried her outside, threw her on his horse, and rode away with her.

But, he hadn't gone very far when he passed the juniper tree with the little bird in its branches. And the bird cried out,

Coo, coo!

There's blood in the shoe!

The foot's too long,

The foot's too wide,

This is not the proper bride!

Well, the prince heard the bird talking to him. And he stopped, and listened.

(Because, again: birds *talk*, you *listen*.)

He listened to the bird. He turned back and looked at the sister, sitting on the back of his horse. He looked from her long black hair, past her beautiful face, down her beautiful dress, to the golden shoe. And indeed, he saw blood spurting up out of the shoe in big crimson gouts, staining her dress all red.

He thought about it for a moment. And then he said, "Hey! This isn't the right girl either!"

You see? He's a genius.

So the prince turned the horse around, rode back to the house, and said, "Don't you have another daughter?"

Well, the stepfather didn't want to admit it. But the prince insisted, and eventually, Jorinda came out. And as soon as the prince saw her, he knew she was the right one. He gave her the shoe, and she cleaned out all the blood and the chunks of flesh, and then she put it on, right there in front of him. And it fit. Perfectly.

The prince cried out, "MY TRUE BRIDE!" And he picked her up, carried her outside, threw her on his horse, and they rode away together.

And they lived happily ever after.

The End

Well, almost.

You see, as the prince and Jorinda were riding past the juniper tree, the little bird called out again. He called out,

Coo, coo!
No blood in the shoe!
The foot is neither long nor wide,
This one is the proper bride!

And then the little bird flew down and landed on Jorinda's shoulder. And there he sat.

Well, the next day there was a great celebration at the castle, for the prince had found his bride. Everyone in the kingdom was invited, and there was much cheering and carousing and carrying on.

Even the two stepsisters came to the celebration (limping, of course). They embraced Jorinda and wept tears of joy and, in voices dripping with sweetness, simpered, "Oh, dear sister, we are so happy for you! So happy! We love you so, so much!"

Well, Jorinda was not sure what to make of this. After all, it was the first nice thing the girls had ever said to her. But, because they were her sisters, she invited them to come up with her on the great balcony that looked out over the throngs of adoring subjects.

She stood on the balcony, holding hands with the prince

(who was very handsome and, of course, quite clever), waving at her future subjects, with her stepsisters by her side and the little bird still perched on her shoulder.

I strongly recommend that you close your eyes while you read this next paragraph.

And while she and the prince waved and smiled at their subjects, the little bird flew from Jorinda's shoulder to the elder stepsister's shoulder. And there, he leaned over and pecked out the stepsister's left eye. She screamed, but the cheers of the crowd were too loud, and no one could hear her. So the bird hopped to her other shoulder and pecked out her right eye. Then he hopped onto the younger stepsister's shoulders and pecked out her eyes, too.

Yes. Really.

That's what actually happens.

And the last line of the real, Grimm story called "Ashputtle" reads:

And so the stepsisters were punished with blindness to the end of their days for being so wicked and false.

The End

Except, of course, that isn't the end.

I mean, it is the end of the sisters' story. They wandered through the world, weeping, weeping, weeping. Nothing could be as terrible to these two sisters as losing their eyes—for their beauty was hidden from them forevermore. And eventually, after many months of wandering, they stumbled into a dark and forbidding forest, where they were eaten by bears.

But Jorinda's story is not over.

And neither, of course, is Joringel's.

Oh, no. Far from it.

The
Juniper Tree

Once upon a time, a young girl lived in a sumptuous room in the highest turret of a castle, waiting for her wedding to a prince.

She was not entirely sure how she felt about it.

On the one hand, Jorinda was proud. She was going to become the princess of all Grimm. It was strange. It was wonderful. It made her dizzy.

On the other hand, she wasn't sure about this whole marrying-the-prince thing. He was a man, and, really, she was just a little girl. They didn't talk to each other often. They didn't seem to like the same things. And she was pretty sure his father, the king, hated her.

Jorinda spent most of her time in her turret room, playing with the little bird from the juniper tree. He had made a small nest for himself under the eaves of her window, and while he never sang words to her, as he had before, he always kept her company, and chirruped merrily. He almost made her forget about that little grave under the juniper tree and that lonely house. Almost.

She did try to. She pushed those memories way, way down, out of her head, beyond her heart, down into the bottom of her stomach. And, most of the time, she could forget about them. But now and then she would catch a glimpse of a solitary tree on the castle grounds, or a closed door, and she would grow sweaty, and her stomach would slosh and churn as if there were a great deal of water locked inside. She asked the servants to bring her an extra mattress to sleep on. But still she tossed and turned at night.

After a few weeks, Jorinda returned home to have a meal with her family.

When the carriage pulled up, her stepfather greeted her with a vigorous hug. As he held her close, he whispered in her ear, "Come with me to the kitchen, so we can prepare dinner." He held her at arm's length and smiled at her. Around his eyes, Jorinda could see grief and fury.

She followed him into the kitchen. And she followed him

out the back of the kitchen. Then she watched her stepfather open the icebox and draw out a great stew pot.

Jorinda's eyes went wide. Her stepfather turned to her. A grin was stretched nearly to his ears. "Hungry?" The little girl shook her head frantically from side to side. But her stepfather said, "Utter a word about this, and you'll be hanged for certain." And then he carried the stew pot to the stove and lit the fire.

Not much later, Jorinda's mother opened the door to her study. Jorinda flung herself into her mother's arms, and she was about to whisper to her not to eat the stew, when her mother raised her head, sniffing the air. "What is that smell?" she asked, wrinkling up her nose. "What are you cooking in there?"

The stepfather called from the kitchen, "Just a stew, dear!"

"Well," said Jorinda's mother, sniffing the air again, "it smells absolutely, positively delicious!" And she pulled away from Jorinda and went over to the dinner table.

Jorinda stared after her, frozen.

The stepfather brought in the stew, and he called to Jorinda to take her place at the table.

The little girl would not touch the hunks of brown meat in her cracked porcelain bowl. Her mother, on the other hand, picked up her fork, stuck a large chunk of meat with it, and then brought it to her lips.

She stopped.

She saw Jorinda staring at her.

She smiled at her daughter.

And then she shoved the piece of meat into her mouth.

She began to chew it.

She stopped chewing it.

She looked at her husband.

"This stew," she said, with her mouth full, "is *delicious*!"

I'm sorry, but this is exactly what really happened. You can read it in any collection of Grimm's stories.

Still, I'm sorry.

Sorry that it is so awesome.

The mother swallowed her first mouthful and then took another, and another, and another.

"Oh, it's *so* delicious," she said as she ate. "I don't think I've ever tasted such a delicious stew in my entire life!" And she shoveled the stew into her mouth, faster and faster. Soon, she had finished what was in her bowl. She grabbed the stew pot and slid it in front of her.

"Aren't either of you eating?" she asked. "This stew is incredible!" And she scooped the stew straight from the pot into her mouth. "I think I'm going to eat every single drop! I think every single drop was made for me and me alone!" And she snatched the bowls from her husband and daughter and ate their stew, too.

At last, when she had finished, she sat back, grinning, with brownish-red sauce all over her face.

"Well," she said, "that was the best stew I've ever had."

Jorinda stared, her mouth hanging open.

And just then, a bird began to sing outside the window.

It was a little bird, all red, with a white head, sitting in the juniper tree, and it had the most beautiful song. He sang his song again and again. And as he sang, the song began to sound like words. Like these words:

My father, he killed me,

Jorinda cocked her head curiously.

My mother, she ate me,

Jorinda looked around the table. Her mother was enjoying the song.

My sister, Jorinda, buried my bones

'Neath the juniper tree.

Her stepfather seemed distracted by something. He was grimacing.

Kewitt! Kewitt! the bird sang.

What a beautiful bird am I!

The mother clapped her hands. "What a beautiful song! That's the most beautiful song I've ever heard!" She leaped up and ran to the window, just in time to see the bird fly from the juniper tree and over the house.

The bird flew directly to the nearby town. There, the little bird landed on the eave of the goldsmith's shop. And he sang his song again:

My father, he killed me,

My mother, she ate me,

My sister, Jorinda, buried my bones

'Neath the juniper tree.

Kewitt! Kewitt!

What a beautiful bird am I!

The goldsmith heard the song and rushed to the window. "Bird!" he exclaimed (yes, he was talking to a bird). "Bird! That's the most beautiful song I've ever heard! Sing it again!"

But the bird said, "I never sing twice for free. Give me your finest golden chain, and I'll sing it again." (Yes, apparently the bird spoke back.)

So the goldsmith rushed into his house, got the finest golden chain he had—all covered with diamonds and emeralds and rubies—and brought it out to the bird. The bird clasped it in one of its little claws, sang the song again, and flew away.

Next the bird flew to a cobbler's house. He perched on an eave and sang:

> My father, he killed me,
> My mother, she ate me,
> My sister, Jorinda, buried my bones
> 'Neath the juniper tree.
> Kewitt! Kewitt!
> What a beautiful bird am I!

The cobbler instantly burst out of his house. "That's the most beautiful song I've ever heard!" he cried. (Okay, he's talking to a bird, too.) "Bird, will you sing it again?"

But the bird said, "I never sing twice for free. Give me a pair of your prettiest, daintiest shoes, and I'll sing it again."

So the cobbler rushed into his house and brought out a pair of tiny red shoes and handed them to the bird, who took them with his other claw. Then he sang his song again and flew away.

Finally, he came to the mill.

Do you know what a mill is? You don't see them around much anymore, so let me tell you. A mill is where people used to bring their grain to be ground into flour. The grain would be put between two enormous stones. Each stone weighed about as much as a small automobile, and each had a hole in the center that a wooden pole passed through. And men, or donkeys, or oxen, would push the huge stones around and around to grind the grain.

Okay. You needed to know that for the story.

So the bird landed on an eave of the mill and began to sing.

My father, he killed me—

Inside the mill, ten men pushed the giant stone wheels around a great wooden dowel, grinding the grain into flour.

My mother, she ate me—

Two men stopped pushing the millstones and listened.

My sister, Jorinda, buried my bones—

Two more men stopped pushing the millstones. The other six men grunted and groaned under the strain of turning the enormous wheels.

'Neath the juniper tree.

Two more men stopped pushing. The other men could barely move the stones now.

Kewitt! Kewitt!

Two more men stopped to listen to the song.

ADAM GIDWITZ

What a beautiful bird am I!

The last two men could no longer move the stones an inch. They heard the final notes of the song. They threw open the windows of the mill. "That was the most beautiful song we've ever heard," they cried (because apparently everyone in this town talks to birds). "Will you sing it again?"

And the bird said, "I never sing twice for free. Give me one of your millstones, and I'll sing it again."

Now, the millstones belonged to the miller. They weren't the men's to give. But they wanted to hear the song again so badly that all ten of them bent their legs and heaved a millstone onto their shoulders and staggered with it out the great wooden doors of the mill. The bird bent his little head and the men slipped the hole at the center of the wheel right over it, so the bird had the giant millstone around his neck.

How, you might ask, did a tiny bird support a millstone that weighed as much as a small automobile?

That's a good question.

My answer? I have no clue.

He just did.

So get over it.

The bird sang the song for the miller's men again. And then he flew back to the house with the juniper tree.

The little bird flew around and around the house, singing his song. Inside, the stepfather and mother and the little girl still sat at the table.

My father, he killed me, the bird sang.

The stepfather suddenly felt as if an arrow had pierced his heart. "I don't feel so well," he said.

My mother, she ate me.

"Do you hear that song?" Jorinda's mother cried. "It's the most beautiful song I've ever heard!"

My sister, Jorinda, buried my bones

'Neath the juniper tree. . . .

Jorinda felt hot tears pressing at the corner of her eyes. She blinked madly. *Choke them back*, she thought.

Kewitt! Kewitt!

What a beautiful bird am I!

And the bird sang the song again.

My father, he killed me . . .

The stepfather slid out of his chair and onto the floor under the table. "I feel like the world is coming to an end!" he said. "I think I'm dying! I can't see!"

My mother, she ate me . . .

"I have to go outside!" the mother cried. "I have to see the bird that sings this beautiful song!"

She leaped from her chair and burst out of the door. As soon as she was outside, the bird opened one of his claws and let fall the golden chain—and it fell directly around the mother's neck. She took one look at it and ran back inside. "Look what the bird gave me!" she cried. "A beautiful golden chain!"

My sister, Jorinda, buried my bones . . .

Jorinda was now blind from the tears she would not let fall. "Maybe I should go outside, too," she sniffled. And she stood up and walked to the door. She emerged into the twilight, wiping her eyes hard, and the bird immediately dropped the two red shoes before her. Without so much as a pause, she slipped out of her own and stepped into them, and suddenly her heart was light. She ran back into the house. "Look what the bird gave me!" she cried.

'Neath the juniper tree . . . the bird sang.

The stepfather was cowering under the table. He began to moan, "Oh, I feel like the world is coming to an end! I feel like I'm burning in the fires of Hell!" Suddenly, he cried, "I can't breathe! Air! Give me air!" And he threw the table over, sending the stew pot and all the plates clattering to the floor, and burst out of the house.

Kewitt! Kewitt! the bird sang.

And as the stepfather came clear of the door—

BANG!

The bird dropped the millstone right on his head.

And it sang, *What a beautiful bird am I!*

The mother and little Jorinda ran outside to see what had caused the great thudding, crunching noise.

They saw the millstone, lying in the center of the yard. The smell of sulfur and brimstone rose from its center.

And beside the stone stood Joringel. As good as new.

"Oh!" his mother said. "You're back!" And then she said, "Now, where did your stepfather get to?"

But Joringel had no chance to answer.

For Jorinda ran at her brother and threw her arms around him and held him so tight he could not breathe.

Their mother scratched her head and started looking all around the grounds for her husband.

Little Jorinda and little Joringel held each other for a long, long time. Neither said a word.

At last, Joringel withdrew and looked at his sister. "If you won't leave me," he whispered, "I won't leave you."

ADAM GIDWITZ

And Jorinda—hesitated.

Just for a moment.

And in that moment, they heard the sound of hooves. They turned. The prince, tall, strong, handsome, and very, very clever, rode up to them.

"Well, my dear," he said, "are you ready to go back to the castle?"

The little boy looked at the prince, and then he looked at his sister.

Jorinda said, "Prince, this is my brother."

The prince squinted at the little boy. "He's not very tall," he said. Which had nothing to do with anything. And then he reached down, picked up the little girl, and put her on the back of his horse.

"Wait," Jorinda said.

The prince waited.

She looked down at Joringel. Her arms were around the prince's waist. She glanced over at her mother, peering in the bushes for her vanished stepfather. She looked at the house. She looked at the juniper tree. She looked back at her brother. She felt a stabbing pain in her back—as if she had just lain down on a sharp stone.

"I'm sorry," she said. "I can't stay here. I just—I can't."

And without any further warning, the prince spurred the horse, and they galloped away.

Jorinda turned and waved at her brother.

Joringel did not wave back.

He just stared.

Why?

Why would she do this?

Well, maybe we'll understand it if we assess the facts for a moment:

Fact 1: Jorinda's mother ignores and neglects her.

Fact 2: Her stepfather and stepsisters were really, really mean to her.

Fact 3: She *killed her brother*. Or at least, she thought she did.

Fact 4: Her mother ate her brother in a stew.

Fact 5: Her brother turned into a bird, pecked out their stepsisters' eyes, and killed their stepfather.

Fact 6: Now a prince wants to take her away from this insane and terrifying home and make her a princess.

So I understand her thinking.

On the other hand, she promised Joringel she wouldn't leave him.

And she is leaving him.

So I understand how he feels, too.

The Three
Hanging Men

Once upon a time, there was a little boy who was having trouble sleeping.

Joringel tossed and turned, as if a stone were lodged under his mattress, until his bedsheets strangled him and he went flailing to the floor. Then he sat on the floor and thought about his stepsisters, who had been blinded by a bird, and his stepfather, who had been crushed by a millstone. (The boy had some vague feeling he'd had something to do with both of these events, but he wasn't sure how that was possible.)

Then he crawled back in bed and thought about his sister, who had said she would never, ever leave him. Which made him toss and turn and fight his twisted bedsheets some more.

And then he heard his mother trudge up the creaky stairs of their little house, sigh, and close the door to her room. It had been three days since his sister had gone away and his stepfather had been crushed by a millstone, and he had not seen his mother once. She spent all her time in her study with her precious books. He wondered what was so special about them. Whatever it was, it was obviously more special than Joringel.

She took wisdom from them. She took solace in them.

Suddenly, Joringel threw his bedsheets to the floor.

If she could, so could he.

Joringel crept down the creaking stairs, until he stood just outside of his mother's study, staring at the doorknob that he had never dared turn. He put his hand on it. It was cool and smooth. He sucked in his breath, turned the knob, and pushed the door open.

The windows were like black paintings, it was so dark outside. But inside the study, one oil lamp, housed in a glass globe, burned faintly on. The floorboards creaked as Joringel approached the nearest wall of books. He could see very few titles—most of the old volumes' names had long faded away. Joringel tilted an old book from the shelf and peered at its cover. *Flubelhoffer's History of the Rhenish Farmer: A Glossary.* Joringel didn't know what that meant, so he let it slide back into place and tipped out another.

Professor Weiner Frankfurter: The Collected Letters, Volume 63.
The boy wondered how the collected letters of someone named Weiner Frankfurter could be important enough to have sixty-three volumes. Then he saw, at the very bottom of the shelf, an enormous, leather-bound book with metal brackets on the spine. He knelt down and tipped it back. It slid right out of its spot and thudded to the floor. The whole house shook. The little boy froze.

Upstairs, he could hear his mother roll over in bed. Joringel did not move. He did not breathe.

Silence fell again.

As carefully as he could, Joringel leaned over the massive tome. The title read, *Extraordinary Plants of Great Power*, by F. Johannes.

Plants? Not interesting, the boy thought. *Great power? More so.*

He opened the book. The hinges that bound the cover to the spine creaked. Joringel froze again and listened for movement upstairs. The only sound was the sputtering and snapping of the oil lamp in its globe. Joringel took the delicate pages between two fingers and began to turn them. He passed the title page. He passed a long introduction about the author's important post as adviser to a king.

At last, he came to an illustration. It was of a green plant with long, slender leaves and little red flowers. The title read "Blood Blossom." Under the title was an explanation of where to find said flower—some mountains south of the kingdom of Märchen, wherever that was—and then there was a description of what the flower could be used for. *"Staunching bleeding, inducing bleeding, making designs and patterns out of bleeding."* The little boy didn't know what *staunching* or *inducing* meant, and he had no interest in making patterns out of blood. He turned the page.

On the next page, there was a sketch of a wide, flat, brown fungus, growing among the roots of a stout tree. The fungus, apparently, was called Swamp Volcano, and the only explanation on the page read *"Caution: If ingested, explosive defecation and emesis will ensue."* Joringel didn't know what defecation and emesis were, but he certainly didn't want to explode. So he turned the page again.

If you, on the other hand, are curious to know what defecation and emesis are, you're going to have to look them up. I'm certainly not going to tell you.

And I recommend you don't ask any adults, either. Because if you do, they will ask why you want to know. And

ADAM GIDWITZ

then you will have to tell them that you read about "explosive defecation and emesis" in this book. At which point, they will take the book away from you.

The oil lamp was nearly out now. Its orange glow illuminated the room one moment and then cast the chamber in darkness the next. The little boy peered at the illustration in front of him. There was a pine tree. Its needles looked deep blue in the darkness. An arrow, drawn in ink, indicated the underside of the branches, and an ornate circle highlighted little berries that looked for all the world like drops of blood. The little boy caught his breath and leaned in. The page read "Juniper Tree Berries," and below those words, this: "Consume with caution. If eaten fresh from the bough on a night of no moon the moment before dawn, all feelings of fear will be eliminated. Duration varies. Side effects can include sudden idiocy."

Just as Joringel read those words, the oil lamp sputtered one last time and died. His heart was pounding. "All feelings of fear will be eliminated." His breath was shallow and quick. He stood and went to the window. He peered outside. The juniper tree stood in the darkness. No moon illuminated its branches.

Joringel walked through the house, out the back door, and

into the garden. The stars shimmered tiny above him. The wind was gentle but chill, and the grass already dewy. He made his way to the dark boughs of the tree. He looked over his shoulder, to the east. The blackness had given way, just, to the deepest blue.

"The fewer feelings I have, the better," Joringel said under his breath. And he reached up and took a little red berry between his fingers. He plucked it down. He closed his eyes.

He put it in his mouth and burst the bitter berry between his teeth.

"And so it begins," came a voice from the darkness.

Joringel's eyes flew open.

"Are you sure it's him?" This was another voice.

The little boy looked all around. He saw no one. His head felt very strange.

"I'm sure," said the first voice.

"Wait, who?" This was someone new. "Who are we talking about again?"

The first voice sighed. "The boy. You know. The special one. With the sister."

"He doesn't look very special to me," said the second voice.

"I still don't know who you're talking about," said the third.

At last, the little boy found them. They were sitting on a low branch of the juniper tree. And they were not human.

They were bird.

Raven, to be precise.

Joringel should have been shocked. He knew he should have been. There were ravens—*talking*. And talking about *him*, no less. But shock originates somewhere in your chest, just below your heart and just above your stomach. And at that moment, that part of Joringel was being occupied by strange gurglings and tinglings that had begun just after he'd swallowed the juniper berry. So he didn't feel shocked at all. He just said, "I'm special?"

The three ravens looked at him all at once. Their small eyes were so perfectly black that they reflected the stars overhead.

"Yes," said the first raven.

"Well, you will be," said the second. "As will your sister."

"I," said the third, "still have no idea what they're talking about."

"That makes two of us," Joringel replied.

The ravens chuckled.

"You have just ingested the berry of a juniper tree, have you not?" asked the first raven.

"I don't know what ingested means," said the little boy, "but if it means ate, then yes, I did."

"Quite so," replied the first raven. "Would you be surprised to learn that you are soon to undertake historic feats of courage and heroism?"

"I don't know what you just said," Joringel replied.

"It's not the right kid," the second raven interjected. "I don't believe it."

"WHAT KID?" the third raven squawked.

"Shall we test my hypothesis?" the first asked.

"I don't know what you just said again," answered Joringel.

"It's not him," the second raven sighed.

"I DON'T KNOW WHAT WE'RE TALKING ABOUT!" screamed the third raven.

The first raven ignored him. "Little boy, would you like to begin the greatest adventure in the history of the Storied Kingdoms?"

Joringel had no idea what the Storied Kingdoms were. But his answer, without any question, was yes.

"Then follow us," said the raven. And he dove from the branch and swooped past Joringel. The second raven swooped down after him. But the third, with a flutter of wings, hopped down onto Joringel's shoulder.

"Do you have any idea what's going on?" the raven asked. Joringel shook his head. "Okay," the black bird replied. "Then let's find out." And he took off after his brothers.

Joringel glanced back at the little house he had grown up in.

A lump formed in his throat.

But he turned away, following the flight of the three ravens into the bloody, rising sun.

They had walked for nearly a day. Once, the third raven had asked him if he found it strange that birds could talk.

"Usually, you kids find it strange," the raven added.

Indeed, Joringel felt that he *should* find it strange. He just didn't. That place between his heart and his chest still tingled, and his head felt like it was swimming in brine.

As the day waned and the gray sky gave way to dusk, the strange party arrived in a dark wood.

"Now let's see if that juniper berry works," announced the first raven.

The trees were blackened and moldy. Their branches were bare, hanging at odd angles like broken, burned bones. As the muddy ground squelched under the little boy's feet, he wondered why he was not frightened. He should have felt frightened. The wind suddenly whipped through the wood, and it moaned, long and low and mournful. Then it fell silent again. This was a place of death.

"Well, I'm scared," said the third raven.

"What do you have to be scared of?" demanded the second. "It's not like you can die."

The little boy cocked his head. "You can't die?"

"There are some things we do, and some things we do not do," replied the first raven. "Dying is of the latter group."

But the third raven said, "Dying isn't the only thing to be afraid of."

"Oh, really?" asked the second.

"Right!" said the third. "There's snakes."

The second raven rolled his black eyes.

"Fire."

He rolled them again.

"Spiders! Spiders are scary."

"You eat spiders!" retorted the second raven.

"Serves them right for scaring me!"

Suddenly a branch cracked and came tumbling through the trees. It landed with a heavy thud not three feet from the little boy.

"That could have killed me," Joringel said aloud. Strangely, the fact did not seem to bother him.

"Keep moving," announced the first raven. He flew from tree to tree, perching for a few moments to let the boy's short legs keep up. His brothers followed suit.

"Falling branches scare me, it turns out," continued the third raven. "I didn't know that until just now."

They flew on.

"Drowning scares me. And sharks. Sharks scare me."

"You've never been in the water!" exclaimed the second raven. "How could you be scared of something that lives where you will never, ever go?"

"Talent," replied the third raven. "And a prodigious imagination. I'm also scared of goblins and dragons and mean fairies. And dog bites. And cat bites. And bug bites."

The air grew colder as the party went deeper and deeper into the wood. The ground became softer and squelchier. The trees thinned under the graying, darkling sky.

"I'm scared of getting hit by a carriage or a train or a bus."

"What's a train?" asked the little boy, still not at all bothered by the forbidding wood.

"I'm scared of flying in airplanes."

"That's ridiculous! Why would you ever go in an airplane? You can fly yourself!" cried the second raven.

"I don't think I would feel very comfortable in a submarine either. I get claustrophobic." Joringel didn't understand anything the ravens were saying.

"Oh, and I'm scared of birds."

"WHAT?"

"That Hitchcock movie *The Birds* really bothered me. And ever since, birds have made me uncomfortable."

"That is the stupidest thing I have ever—"

"Quiet," the first raven commanded. "We're here."

They stood in the barren, dark heart of the wood. The wind moaned angrily in the trees, and the mist enveloped them like a funeral shroud.

"Where's here?" asked the second raven, squinting at his surroundings.

The first raven intoned, "We are in the wood at the edge of Mörder Swamp."

The third raven said, "Murder Swamp? Spelled *M-U-R-D-E-R*?"

The first raven laughed. "No! Of course not! That would be creepy. It's spelled *M-Ö-R-D-E-R*."

"Oh," the third raven sighed, relieved.

"Wait," said the second, "isn't *Mörder* just German for 'murder'?"

"What? Oh. Yes. Technically," agreed the first.

"Right," said the third. "So I'm terrified."

The first raven turned to Joringel. "Do you think that you could spend a night here all by yourself?"

Joringel glanced around at the rotting branches, the thick, wet mud, the cold, drifting mist. Somewhere, a wolf howled. He shrugged. "Why not?"

ADAM GIDWITZ

"You wouldn't be afraid?" asked the first raven.

"I would be afraid," interjected the third.

"Yeah," said the second, "we've established that."

Again, Joringel shrugged. "I don't think I know how anymore."

The first raven gave the second raven a knowing glance. So the second raven said, "Well, let him try it."

"Can I build a fire?" Joringel inquired. "It is a bit cold."

"Sure," the first raven replied.

"Do *we* have to stay here?" asked the third raven.

"The whole point," said the first raven, "is that we leave the boy alone."

"Oh! Good!"

The first raven said, "We'll be back in the morning." And with that, he flew away. The second raven followed him. The third raven, sitting on a stump in the middle of the eerie clearing, stared wonderingly at the little boy. Suddenly, he shook himself and looked around. His brothers were gone.

"WAIT!" he cried. "WAIT FOR ME!" And he went flying out of the clearing after them.

The clearing in which Joringel stood was dominated by one enormous tree. Its bark was black and rotted, and worms seethed over its soft surface.

The air was cold, and getting colder, so Joringel set out among the trees to collect wood and kindling. And while any other child—no, any person at all—would have jumped as branches popped under his feet, as wolves cried in the distance, and as bats screeched overhead, little Joringel was not afraid. He did not, it appeared, remember how to be.

He brought the wood and kindling back to the clearing and began to make a flame with a little flint box he kept in his pocket. When the fire had sparked into life, its yellow light danced against the trunk of the great tree under which he stood.

At which point, Joringel noticed three shadows. Shadows that seemed to sway back and forth upon the branches of the trees. His eyes followed the shadows up, and up, and up.

And there he saw, hanging from a branch, three men. Ropes were tied around their broken necks, and their feet dangled lifelessly.

"*No!*" whispered the third raven, who was hiding, with his brothers, in a tree not very far away.

"Shh!" hissed the first. "Just watch."

Joringel put his hands on his hips and stared at the three hanging men.

"What are you doing up there?" he called.

They didn't answer. Being dead and all.

The third raven looked inquiringly at the second. The second shrugged his black shoulders.

Joringel sat down by the fire. But he kept glancing up at the three dead men. They swung slowly this way and that, their ropes creaking in the darkness.

And then Joringel said, "I bet they're cold. I should let them come sit by my fire."

"WHAT?" cried the third raven.

"SHHH!" hissed the first.

The little boy called up to the three hanging men. "Hey! Do you want to come down and sit by the fire."

"What is going on?" the third raven demanded.

The first smiled. "'Side effects can include sudden idiocy.'"

"They must not be able to hear me up there," Joringel announced. So he got to his feet, walked to the base of the tree, and began to climb it.

"No . . ." murmured the third raven.

Insects crawled over the little boy's hands and his face. He tossed them off carelessly. Pieces of rotting wood crumbled in his grip, sending him sliding back down the trunk. He just climbed up again. His fingers dug into seething swarms of worms. The little boy didn't mind.

He clambered up to the branch with the dead men and said, "Hey! Do you want to come sit by the fire?" The men's heads lay at unnatural angles on their shoulders, and their thick blue tongues stuck out of their mouths.

"Maybe they're too cold to answer me," Joringel said. So he took a little knife out of his pocket and cut through the three ropes.

Thunk!

Thunk!

Thunk!

The three men dropped to the ground. Joringel shimmied back down the tree, ignoring the spiders creeping down his shirt.

The three men were splayed on the earth now, their legs and arms all twisted, their necks crooked and bruised. The boy tut-tutted them for being so lazy. He began to sit them up all around the fire.

"I can't watch!" cried the third raven, covering his face with a black wing. The second raven winced to see the boy handling the broken corpses. But the first raven just smiled and shook his head wonderingly from side to side.

At last, the little boy had managed to get all the dead men sitting up around the fire. He took his place beside them. He tried to make conversation, but they would not respond. At first, he thought they were being rude. But then he figured it was their thick blue tongues sticking out of their mouths that made them so quiet. He leaned over to one of them and tried to push his tongue back in his mouth.

Just then, the man across the fire from Joringel started to sway. He swayed, back and forth, back and forth. And then, *whoomph*. He toppled over, headfirst, into the fire.

All three ravens screamed. Quietly.

"Whoa!" cried Joringel, leaping to his feet. The man's head had caught on fire. Flames danced all over his skull and shoulders. "Get up, get up!" the boy cried. He pulled the man out of the fire and hit the flames on his head until they went out.

"I do not believe what I am seeing," murmured the third raven.

But just then, another of the men began to sway, back and forth, back and forth. And then, *whoomph*. He toppled over into the fire, too.

"Whoa! Stop that!" Joringel cried. Flames danced up and down the man's skull. The little boy pulled the man up and beat the flames out. At which point, the third man fell over. His head caught fire, too.

The ravens' beaks all hung open limply.

Joringel put his hands on his hips. "If you guys don't know

how to sit around a fire properly, I'm just going to tie you back up in that tree. Is that what you want?"

The two men whom Joringel had already rescued began to sway again, back and forth, back and forth, almost as if they were nodding. And then they both toppled over, face-first, into the fire. Their heads burst into flames.

All three ravens covered their eyes.

"Right, that's it!" cried Joringel. So he dragged all three men out of the fire, beat the flames out, hauled them back up the tree, and tied them back to their branch. Then he shimmied down, sat himself under their creaking ropes, and began to pick spiders from his hair and centipedes from his clothes.

"Well," said the third raven, "that was the most upsetting thing I have ever seen in my life."

And the second raven replied, "Yes. Yes it was."

"Shall we go retrieve the boy?" asked the first raven.

"To be honest," answered the third, "now I'm kind of scared of him, too."

"Yeah, I'm with my brother," added the second.

But they flew down and landed on the ground by Joringel's feet.

"So," asked the first raven, "how's it going so far?"

"Boring," said Joringel.

The three ravens stared.

And then the first raven said, "Hey, you think the juniper berry is something? You should check out this castle I know. You'll love it." And with that, he took a loping, raven hop and leaped into the air. His brothers followed him.

And so did Joringel.

Malchizedek's Mansion

Once upon a time, a little girl lived in a tiny room in the highest turret of the Castle Grimm.

Not only was the room tiny, but it was drafty, too. And sparsely decorated. Hardly the accommodations you would expect for a future princess.

Jorinda sat on the small bed in her tiny room and worried.

She worried about the king. She was pretty sure he hated her. Every time she spoke, he scoffed. Every time she made a mistake, he laughed. Every time the prince smiled at her, the king rolled his eyes.

She was also worried about the prince. Yes, he was handsome and tall and strong. And yes, everyone said he was very clever (though Jorinda had never seen any evidence of this). But he never had very much to say to her. And besides, he was an adult. And she, it had to be admitted, was a little girl.

Finally, she was worried about her brother. She kept picturing him standing in their garden, staring at her, as she rode away with the prince. She tried to stop thinking about it. And also about her mother, closed in her study. And also about the not-very-clever prince. And the king who hated her. She tried to not think about a lot of things.

With all this not thinking about things, she was not sleeping very well at night.

In a grand room at the heart of the grand castle, the king paced the floor in grand, dizzying circles.

"She can't marry him," he muttered. "She can't, she can't, she can't, she can't."

"Why can't she marry me, father?" the prince pouted. The prince pouted often. It was not very becoming for a young man the prince's age. But he did it anyway. "Why not?"

"*Why not?*" the king bellowed. "Because she's a *child*! And a *servant*! And they call her *Toilet Cleaner*! How do you think you'll look introducing your wife to your allies? Or worse, to your rivals?" Then the king adopted a vacant expression and said,

"'How do you do, King Vlad of the Tartars? I am the king of all Grimm, and this is my wife, Toilet Cleaner.' *Does that sound good to you?*"

The prince looked at the floor. His shoulders went up and down.

"And stop pouting," the king added. "You're a grown man, for heaven's sake."

The prince crossed his arms and looked out the window. It was not that the prince liked the girl they called Ashputtle very much. He had found her very enchanting in her blood-red gown at the ball. But now? She was a little girl who didn't make him feel quite so clever as everyone said he was. Still, he didn't like to be told he couldn't have something. Even if he didn't want it.

A servant came into the room. He had a long scroll of parchment over his arm.

"What?" the king snapped.

"The tax lists, your majesty."

The king grunted. "Everyone paying?"

"There's a small matter of adjusting the value of Lord Lewes's land holdings that border Mörder Swamp—"

"Just take care of it."

"Very good, sir. And of course," the servant went on, "Malchizedek isn't paying."

"Of course," said the king, waving a lazy hand. "He never does." But then the king stopped. "Wait a minute."

"Your majesty?"

"Malchizedek isn't paying?"

"No, sir. As you say, he never does."

The king smiled. "No, he never does."

"And we have tried countless times to make him pay."

"We *have* tried countless times, haven't we?" The king grinned.

"But the tax collectors keep—"

"Dying," the king said. "They keep dying, don't they?"

"Yes, your majesty. He kills them."

The king was smiling beatifically, staring at the ceiling and stroking his long brown beard. "He does, doesn't he?"

The carriage rattled along a rocky track, hugging the side of the cliff.

The little girl stared out the window, across a great crevasse. At the bottom of this crevasse, a dozen shattered carriages were littered among the stones. Jorinda held on to her seat with white knuckles. Across the crevasse, sitting at the top of a rocky promontory, stood a tall, sinister black house.

"That's it," the king said. "Malchizedek's place."

———

Okay, if I'm going to keep talking about Malchizedek, you probably ought to learn how to pronounce his name.

It's Mal-KEE-zuh-deck.

Just what you were saying, right?

Jorinda, gazed at the dark windows and rotting shutters. "And I just have to ask Mr. Malchizedek to pay his taxes?"

"That's it!" the king replied. "But he doesn't like to pay. So I'm going to drop you off there and let you stay the night. See if you can't convince him."

"Did he invite me?"

"Invite you? Ah . . . well . . . no. But he won't mind, I'm sure."

Jorinda returned to gazing out of the carriage window at the dark house. It was the most inaccessible, inhospitable house she had ever laid eyes on. She thought, maybe, he would mind.

"Why won't he pay?"

"Oh, some poppycock about land confiscation and eminent domain and other complicated terms you wouldn't understand."

Jorinda nodded and continued staring at the great, dark house.

Malchizedek wasn't there.

No one answered their knock at the door. So three men of the king's guard broke the lock and knocked the door in. They searched the house, but there was no sign of him.

"Don't worry," said the king. "He typically only comes out at night."

"That's strange," said Jorinda.

"Not really," replied one of the guards. "Ogres typically only come out at night."

"Wait, what?" The little girl started. "He's an ogre?"

"You'll find out for yourself soon enough!" The king smiled. "We'll be back for you in the morning. Probably." And with that, he led his guards out the front door. An instant later, the little girl heard the carriage begin its long, rattling trip back across the cliff face to the Castle Grimm.

And now begins one of the strangest, freakiest, most twisted stories the Brothers Grimm ever told.

If you are a fan of strange, freaky, twisted stories, I believe you will like this one.

If you are not a fan of strange, freaky, twisted stories, may I ask you, *Why are you reading this book?*

The little girl stood in the middle of a large room. Light slanted in through the windows hazily. White sheets lay on all the furniture, and enormous cobwebs stretched from the corners of the ceiling to the floor.

"Hello?" she called. "Hello?"

No answer.

So Jorinda sat down in the center of the black floor, under the black ceiling, surrounded by white-sheeted furniture, and taking a small sewing kit from her pocket to pass the time, she waited for night to fall.

When the sun's rays disappeared from the window frames and the sky over the rocky landscape outside the mansion grew dusky blue, the little girl rose and started a fire in the great fireplace. Then she sat back down with her sewing and waited for Malchizedek.

The house made strange noises. Creaks and whines. Clanks and shuffles. Jorinda wondered if it was the ogre, moving around his house. But the sounds came from upstairs and downstairs, to her left and to her right all at once. Strange indeed.

Finally, the last light was extinguished from the sky. The small fire, crackling and popping in the grate, was the only light in the whole house—and probably for many miles around. Jorinda felt cold. She began to shiver.

And at that moment, she noticed something she had not seen before.

Off in a far corner of the room, two eyes flashed at her. They looked like cat eyes—incandescent and almond-shaped. But they were not green, nor yellow, like most cat eyes. They were crimson. And they blazed like fire.

"Hello?" the little girl said.

The eyes blazed on.

"There's nothing to be afraid of," she whispered to herself. She rose to her feet and walked gingerly toward the cat. "Here, kitty, kitty," she murmured. "Here, kitty."

"Meow," replied the cat.

Jorinda smiled.

And then the smile slid from her face.

For as she approached the cat, she saw that it was no typical housecat. It was a panther, a jaguar, a black tiger—a great, fearsome, jungle beast.

"Here, kitty?" she tried once more.

And then the kitty pounced.

Jorinda screamed and threw herself backward, sliding across the floor. The great black cat landed just before her, gnashing humongous teeth in slavering jaws. Jorinda pulled herself back, and back, and back, and the great black cat followed her, hissing, its silky coat rippling with hidden power, its fiery eyes flashing.

And then the cat leaped at her again. Jorinda prepared to die.

Suddenly, the beast froze in midair. It made a choking, hissing sound. And then it crashed to the floor.

The great cat was straining, straining to get at Jorinda. But it made no progress. And then Jorinda noticed a chain, thick and black, extending from the beast's neck back to the wall. She wanted to cry with relief.

Until she saw the eyes behind her.

These, too, flashed red like fire and were joined by growling and snarling. And then, from the darkness, leaped an enormous, monstrous dog. It had a thick, matted black coat, huge foaming jaws, and teeth like knives. Jorinda screamed and pulled herself away from it. But in so doing, she was approaching the great cat again.

The cat reached for her with its long claws, hissing and swiping at the air. Jorinda jumped away. The great dog snarled and snapped. She jumped away from that. The beasts' eyes burned like flames.

There was a single place, right in the center of the room, where the girl could stand and neither the cat nor the dog could reach her. So she stood in that spot, hyperventilating, trying not to pass out.

And then there were more eyes. Pairs of fiery eyes all around the room.

Jorinda decided to scream.

She screamed and screamed and screamed at the top of her lungs, and more huge black beasts—bears and wolves and wolverines—leaped from the walls, their eyes blazing, their jaws snapping, their claws swiping.

As the beasts flew through the air toward her, the little girl said to herself, "I am about to be dead."

But, all at once, all of the black beasts stopped in midair and crashed to the wooden floorboards. They, too, were on chains. If Jorinda stood as straight as a board and as still as a stone, directly in the center of the room, not one of them could reach her with jaw or claw.

And so Jorinda remained in that one spot, not moving, barely breathing—as a dozen slavering red-eyed beasts snarled and snapped and growled and hissed within inches of her flesh.

ADAM GIDWITZ

All she had to do was buckle with fear, collapse from fatigue, or try to escape, and she would die.

So she did the only thing she could do.

She closed her eyes and waited.

Six hours later, the first ray of sun shot through a cobwebbed windowpane. At that very instant, all of the slavering, growling, yowling, hissing, snapping, biting, murderous creatures instantly disappeared.

At which point, Jorinda passed out.

Not long thereafter, the door opened. The king poked his head in.

"*Is she dead?*" someone whispered.

The king's eyes roved over the room. He started. Jorinda was sitting by the fireplace, sewing. "How—" he stammered, "how are you still alive?"

The little girl shrugged. "Why wouldn't I be alive?" She stood up and stretched her legs.

The king shook his head like he was seeing things. "Malchizedek didn't kill you? I was pretty sure he would kill you."

"He didn't kill me."

"He's killed all the others."

"Oh," said Jorinda. "Interesting."

"Well? Did he agree to pay?"

Jorinda shook her head. "I didn't see him. But I played with his pets. They were cute."

The king peered at her curiously. Then he said, "If you didn't see him, you must stay here again tonight. We've got to have those taxes."

Jorinda gritted her teeth and pretended to smile.

As the king was leaving, he turned and looked at the little girl one last time. She kept smiling. The king shook his head in wonder and closed the door.

Jorinda stared after him. She should leave. She should run away on the mountain track and try to find her way to the kingdom.

But where would she go? The king wouldn't let her come back to the castle, would he? And she wouldn't go home. Not after what had happened there. No matter how terribly she missed Joringel. Besides, she decided, if she could get Malchizedek to pay, the king would have to let her become the princess of all Grimm.

Jorinda set her jaw, buckled her heart into a tiny little ball, and got back to her sewing.

———

ADAM GIDWITZ

I don't know about you, but if I were Jorinda, I would do the sensible thing and run away screaming right about now.

That night, when the last light of the sun disappeared from the window frame, Jorinda saw no flaming eyes in the corners. And she looked for them. Believe me.

So she sat sewing by the fire. Again, strange sounds came from the house around her. There was creaking and scraping, dragging and shuffling, and again it all seemed to come from above and below and to the left and to the right. Jorinda's skin was crawling.

And then she heard the words, "Help me!"

She sat straight up. The words were quiet. But desperate.

"Help me!"

They seemed to be coming from the chimney.

"Help me!"

Jorinda stood, went to the fireplace, and peered up the chimney. She could see nothing but darkness.

"Help me!"

Whoever or whatever it was, it was certainly up there. So Jorinda grabbed the flue handle, which opens and closes the chimney, and gave it a hard turn to the left. Then she gave it a hard turn to the right. Then she gave it a hard turn to the left again.

With a loud crash, the fire exploded, spewing ash and dust everywhere.

Jorinda staggered backward, covering her face and choking. Finally, the cinders settled, and she was able to wipe the soot from her face and look.

Crawling away from the fire was half a man.

It was the top half. He had no hair at all, no clothes, bulging eyes, and vaguely green skin. He was pulling himself forward by his fingernails, out of the fire, into the room. And he was moaning, "Help me! Help me! Help me!"

Jorinda backed away.

"Help me!" he moaned. He dragged himself toward her. "Help me!"

"How can I help you?" she asked. She could not stop staring at the torn and tattered flesh just below his belly button—where his body ended.

"Help me!" He dragged himself slowly after her. She moved to the left, to get out of his way.

He followed her.

She moved to the right.

He followed her.

"Help me!" he cried. "Help me!"

"How?" asked Jorinda. "How? Tell me how!"

And then the fireplace exploded with dust and ash again, and when it had cleared and the girl had wiped the soot from her face again, she saw a pair of legs, kicking and dancing in the flames.

"Are those yours?" she asked.

"Help me!"

Clearly they were. They, too, were hairless and naked save for a loincloth, and they too had a sickly green tint. They kicked frantically out of the fire and into the middle of the room.

"Help me!"

"Okay, okay!" she said. "I'll help you." So she walked over to the legs, grabbed them by a foot, and dragged them toward the top half of the man. They kicked and danced as she pulled them, as if they were fighting her. When she got them as near the man's top half as she could, she sat on them. "Come here," she said.

The half man pulled himself toward her, moaning, "Help me!"

Jorinda grabbed him by the arm and flipped him onto his back. Then she yanked his body toward his legs, which she was still sitting on. Finally, she took out her sewing kit.

"Help me!"

"What do you think I'm doing?"

She took out a needle and some very thick thread, and she began to sew the top half of the man to the bottom half. The legs stopped kicking, the arms stopped grasping, but the man kept moaning, "Help me! Help me!"

At last, Jorinda connected the first stitch to the last stitch and tied the thread off with a sturdy knot.

"There," she said. "All done."

The pale green man with no hair and wide eyes stared at her. And then he said, "Thank you."

She smiled at him.

And then he said, "Now I am going to kill you."

"What?" she cried.

The man's green, hairless arms snapped closed around Jorinda's body, and his muscular hands grabbed her by the throat. They were like iron. He squeezed her and squeezed her. She began to choke. She could not breathe. She grabbed his hands and pulled and yanked and pried and kicked. But still she was choking, gagging, suffocating. Her eyes bulged. Her face convulsed. Veins burst in her forehead. Her vision failed.

Her hands dropped to her sides. Still the man strangled her with his iron grip. She was dying. He lifted her into the air and strangled her.

And then, with her very last strength, the fingers on Jorinda's left hand reached into the pocket of her frock, shakingly opened the little sewing kit, and managed to remove a pair of silver scissors. The scissors traveled slowly, tremblingly, out of her pocket and to the man's midsection. There, they found the thick thread that held the two halves of him together, and they cut it.

The scissors fell to the floor. The man continued to crush her windpipe, as if nothing had happened. She was dying. Dying. But, with trembling, convulsing fingers, she took hold of the thick thread, and she pulled. Her legs dangled, she saw nothing but darkness, but she pulled and pulled and pulled.

The man's grip went lax.

Jorinda fell to the ground in a heap.

She lay there and choked and coughed and heaved the sweet air into her lungs. Her throat ached. Her eyes burned. Her nose ran. But she could breathe. She could breathe.

At last, she looked up. The top half of the man was crawling around moaning, "Help me! Help me! Help me!" And his legs kicked and danced in the middle of the floor.

Jorinda got up and stoked the fire. Then she grabbed the man's legs by a heel, and the top of him by a wrist. She dragged them across the room. And then, one after the other, she threw each half of the man into the fire.

"Help me!" he moaned. "Help me!" Jorinda watched the green skin turn black. "Help me! Help me!" His bones crackled in the flames.

By morning, there was nothing left of him.

When the sun was streaming into the room in all of its yellow glory, the king threw the door open and peered inside.

"Well?" he called. "Are you dead yet?"

Jorinda was sitting by the fire. Not sewing. She was done with sewing.

"No!" she called back. "Still alive! Thanks for asking!"

The king came into the house with his guards.

"Did Malchizedek come?"

"No, but his friend did. I helped him with some sewing, and we talked for a while. Then he had to go."

"Oh," said the king, gaping and nodding at the little girl. "Okay."

"I'll wait for him one more night," she informed the king. "But if he doesn't come tonight, I say he doesn't live here anymore, and you can take this place for your summer palace."

"Ah!" smiled the king wanly. "Yes! Good idea!" He backed out of the house, nodding and smiling at Jorinda like he was afraid of her.

———

Jorinda sat in the big dark room with the cobwebs and the sheeted furniture all day. She drummed her fingers on the floor. She stared out the window at the great stone cliffs circling the huge crevasse. She wondered what the night would bring.

At last, the light failed, and, for the third evening in a row, Jorinda got the fire going in the grate. The house made its strange noises—creaks and whines and clanks and the sound of things being dragged around upstairs and downstairs and all around.

And then, the sounds seemed to come together. They seemed to concentrate themselves on the room just next to the one Jorinda was sitting in. They grew louder, and louder, and louder. And then—

BAM! The door to the room slammed open, and standing in it was an enormous, hideous form. Its huge body terminated at the top of its huge, hunching shoulders—which towered over a long scrawny neck, craning out from the body like a vulture's. A bald head with a great white beard, tiny black teeth, and round, red-rimmed eyes was perched at the end of the neck.

It was an ogre.

At least, Jorinda figured it was. She had never seen an ogre before—but when you see one, you just kinda know it.

"Who is in Malchizedek's house?" the ogre boomed.

Jorinda stood up. "Me," she said. And she curtsied.

The ogre strode forward until he was standing directly in front of her. She stood no taller than his waist. He bent his great ugly head to see the little girl.

"Why do you violate my home?" His voice was like war drums.

"I'm very sorry, Mr. Malchizedek, sir," Jorinda stammered, curtsying again. "I'd just like to talk to you for a minute."

"What of?" His breath smelled like rotting fish. His black teeth seemed ready to fall out of his gums. His red-rimmed eyes stared.

Slowly, Jorinda said, "I think you have been wronged."

Malchizedek furrowed his brow. "By whom?"

"The king," she replied.

Malchizedek frowned. Then he said, "Go on."

"He claims you owe him taxes," the small girl continued, peering up at the ogre's enormous, crooked form. "But my guess is you don't."

"Indeed I do not!" boomed Malchizedek.

"He's confiscated your land, I gather?" she continued. "Eminent domain or something?"

"Yes!" bellowed Malchizedek. "Indeed he did!"

And then Jorinda said, "Tell me about it."

So Malchizedek took the white sheets off two of the chairs, pulled them up to the fire, and told her all about it.

"Once, this house stood on a beautiful meadow. It was all grass and trees and sheep grazing peacefully. But then this king, when he was quite young, decided that the Castle Grimm needed to be larger." The ogre rolled his eyes. Jorinda did, too. The ogre smiled approvingly. "He announced that the stone would be quarried from the meadow, for it is well known that the stone in these mountains is the best in all of Grimm." Jorinda nodded as if it was indeed well known. "I protested greatly, for this was my meadow, and it was beautiful. But the king claimed eminent domain, and my beautiful meadow was destroyed."

"Terrible," Jorinda murmured. And she wasn't lying. It did sound terrible.

"So now I refuse to pay the king taxes. Is that so wrong?" The ogre tipped his great, ugly face down to Jorinda's, as if he really wanted to know what she thought.

"No," she said. "It isn't wrong at all."

Malchizedek got a faraway look on his face, and for a long time, no one said anything. And then, quite suddenly, he brought his red-rimmed eyes right up to Jorinda's. "Wait, why are you here?"

Jorinda took a deep breath. Then she explained the whole story. That she was supposed to marry the king's son, that the king didn't like her very much, and that he'd brought her here to be killed.

"That's not what he told me, of course," she added. "He told me to ask you to pay your taxes. But what are the chances that *I* could get *you* to pay your taxes?"

"None."

"He expected you to kill me," Jorinda explained.

"I still might," said Malchizedek.

"Oh"—Jorinda nodded—"I know." And then she added, "But wouldn't you rather have a friend for life living in the castle? First as the princess and then as the queen?"

Malchizedek thought about that for a moment. A sly look crept into his features. "Only," he answered, "if that queen would give me a new house, with a great big meadow. As a gift, of course."

She nodded. "I think the queen might be willing to do that. But first she'd have to get to be queen."

"Of course."

"Which would mean you'd have to pay your taxes until then."

"I see."

"Plus whatever you owe from years past."

The ogre looked at her. For a while he was silent. And then he said, "You're quite an impressive little girl."

"Thank you." She smiled.

And they shook hands.

The king could not believe the size of the sack that Jorinda handed him the next day. It weighed at least twenty pounds. And it was filled entirely with gold coins.

"This should do," she said. "Just leave him alone, and he'll pay every year, right on time."

"How did you do it?" the king demanded. He was gaping at the little girl.

"I just talked to him." She smiled. "That's all."

The king was not happy.

But he was impressed.

And more than a little bit frightened.

Sleeping Beauty

Once upon a time, some years before the tale of Jorinda and Joringel began, a queen gave birth to a baby girl. She was named Briar Rose, and to celebrate her birth, the king and queen held a great feast, and they invited all the great and powerful people of their land. In particular, they invited twelve Wise Women. There were actually thirteen Wise Women in the kingdom, but the king only had twelve golden plates for them to eat from. So one of them had to stay home.

I know. That sounds like a stupid reason not to invite the thirteenth Wise Woman. But that's how the story goes.

Also, sometimes these women are called Fairies, and

sometimes they are called Witches. No one really seems to know what they were.

You call them whatever you want. Call them Zombies in Tutus, if you want. I'm calling them Wise Women.

Well, the feast went splendidly. All the guests gave the infant princess the finest gifts they could think of. At last, it was the Wise Women's turn to bestow their gifts. The first Wise Woman gave the little girl beauty, the second gave her intelligence, the third gave her an impeccable sense of direction, and so on and so forth. The eleventh Wise Woman gave her a blessed childhood, full of happiness and sunshine. The twelfth wise woman had just opened her mouth to bestow her gift, when suddenly the thirteenth Wise Woman swept into the room. She was furious at not having been invited—especially for such a ridiculous reason as a shortage of golden plates; she could have brought her own stupid plate!—so she bellowed, "When this girl has lived for thirteen years, her blessed childhood will end, and she will suddenly sicken, sadden, and mourn. She will feel as if every injury in the world was being done to her and her alone. She will suffer every day of her life!" Then she swept from the hall, muttering, "And get yourself some more stupid plates. . . ."

The guests stared, horror-stricken. But then the twelfth Wise Woman, who had not yet bestowed her gift, stepped forward. "I cannot undo the curse," she said, "but I can soften it. The girl will not suffer every day of her life. Only once a month, for a span of a few days. And then the pain will leave her, and she will be as she ever was."

Well, this was some consolation to the king and queen.

They raised their daughter with all the love in their hearts, until the day of her thirteenth birthday. On that day, the princess sat up in bed and began to weep.

"What's wrong?" her mother asked her.

The little girl tried to explain. There was so much suffering in the world. So much injustice. Every day, beetles were dying and lambs were stillborn and people starved because of a bad rainfall. It wasn't fair. The world was a terrible place. Nothing the queen said made her daughter feel any better. The girl just buried her head in her hands and wept.

The second day after her thirteenth birthday, the girl raged around the castle, breaking things and shouting at people for no reason. Nothing was right. Nothing was good enough. Her father chased after her, begging her to be reasonable. She threw a chamber pot at his head. It had just been used. He left her alone after that.

The third day, she lay in bed and writhed in unbearable pain, and no medicine could ease her suffering.

On the fourth day, the girl felt fine; she passed the month happily. And then the cycle began again.

This happened every month for twelve months. And then, at the beginning of the thirteenth month, the girl wept all through the first day at the horrors of the world, raged all through the second at nothing in particular, and writhed in unbearable agony all through the third.

"Oh, I can't take it!" the girl cried. "I hate my life! I hate it! Make the pain go away! Make it go away!"

Just then, by her bedside, appeared the thirteenth Wise Woman, the one who had not been invited to the feast. "There, there, my dear," said the old crone. "Let me help you."

"How?" the girl begged, writhing in her sweaty sheets. "All the doctors, all the Wise Women, have tried everything! Nothing helps! The world is a terrible place, full of suffering and stupidity and pain!"

"I can make the pain go away," the thirteenth Wise Woman said. "Would you like that?"

"Yes!" the girl cried. "Please make it go away!"

"Do you wish to feel no more sorrow? No more anger?"

"Oh, yes! Please!"

ADAM GIDWITZ

"Never again will you weep at suffering or rage at injustice—"

"That's all I want!"

"Never will the pain of living encroach on your peaceful mind."

"JUST DO IT ALREADY!"

The Wise Woman smiled. "Here," she said. "Take a bite of this apple."

The girl sat up in bed. She looked at the apple—speckled with gold and flashing in the morning light. She grabbed it, took a huge bite, and swallowed without chewing.

Suddenly, she began to choke. She fell back in bed and choked and choked and choked. And then she lay still.

As soon as the girl stopped moving, a deep sleep spread over the entire castle. A banquet was being held in the great hall, and instantly the king, the queen, and all the lords and ladies fell headfirst into their bowls of soup. The horses fell asleep in the stables, the dogs in the courtyard, the pigeons on the roof, and the flies on the wall. Even the fire on the hearth stopped flaming and fell asleep, and the roast stopped crackling, and the cook, who was about to pull the kitchen boy's hair because he had broken all the eggs on the floor, let go and fell asleep. And the wind died down, and not a leaf stirred on the trees.

All around the castle, a thorny briar began to grow. Each

year it grew higher until in the end it surrounded and covered the whole place, and only the tower where the princess slept loomed over the secluded, sleeping valley.

The story of Briar Rose soon spread. From time to time, a knight or a prince came to the castle and tried to pass through the thorny briar. But none succeeded, for the briar bushes clung together as though they had hands, and so young men were caught and couldn't break loose and died a pitiful death.

And so the castle stood, silent and still, in the midst of the thorny thicket, with the slumbering king and queen and lords and ladies and servants—and the princess, lying in her bed in the highest tower.

Many, many years later, the castle stood in its quiet valley, forgotten by time.

Its heavy gray tower loomed in the darkness of the early morning, framed by fading stars and the high hills that surrounded it. But below the tower, the stones of the castle were not framed by stars—but by briars; a thicket of thorns encased the castle like a coffin. Birds flitted out of the briar and away, crying that the morning approached.

Three ravens sat on an abandoned well and stared up at the strange sight.

"What happened to it?" asked the second raven.

"No one knows," said the first.

"Well, we do," said the third.

"Right," said the first. "No one besides us. The story has been lost to the ages."

Joringel stood beside them, gaping. "Do people live in there?"

"Well, in a sense. But no one feels any pain anymore."

Joringel walked up to the thicket. The sky in the east was not so dark as it had been just a moment ago. He tried to peer through the thorny, tangled briar. It was at least half a mile thick.

"No one feels any pain?" Joringel asked. The tingling in his chest was fading, and the feelings that had tormented him at home were growing again like weeds. Images of closed doors and chests of apples and princes on horseback rose before his eyes.

"None at all," replied the first raven. "But the price—"

Joringel cut him off. "I don't care. I want to go in."

"That doesn't seem like a good idea," said the second.

"I think I see a corpse in the thicket over there . . ." began the third.

But Joringel had already slid through a small gap in the thorns and into the briar.

There was no room to walk. Joringel slid and crawled and pulled himself through the thicket. A thorn tore his shirt. Another dragged across his cheek, leaving a ragged red line beaded with dots of blood.

Then he stopped. There was a man ahead of him in the briar. He yanked himself through the thorns, opening a long red gash on the back of his neck. The man was wearing a mail shirt and had a sword raised above his head, as if he was trying to hack the briar to bits. Except that the man was not hacking anything. He stood perfectly still.

Joringel drew himself up beside the man. The sun was just starting to peer over the horizon, its yellow light filtering through the tangle of thorns.

Joringel looked up at the man.

The boy fell backward, trying to push himself away. But there was nowhere to go. The thicket held him and cradled him in a blanket of thorns.

The man's mouth was open, as were his eyes. But his face was locked in the frozen silence of death.

Joringel turned around and pushed on. The sun rose higher. The tingling feeling in Joringel's chest was gone. Sweat began to stand out on the back of his neck, stinging the fresh cut. The briar was becoming even thicker. Joringel had to grab branches of thorns—which punctured his palms—and rip them out of his way. He paused, trying to collect his breath. His muscles burned. Perhaps he should just stay where he was for a while. His eyelids became heavy. Yes, it would be much easier to rest right there . . .

Just then, he noticed another man ahead of him in the thicket. This man was as still as the first, but he was strangely gaunt. Joringel shook the lethargy from his eyes and forced his arms and legs to keep dragging him forward, until he was alongside the man.

Joringel's heart turned in his chest. The man's skin was pulled back so tightly you could make out his skull beneath it. His eyes were shut tight, but his mouth was open, as if he had been screaming. His teeth were blackened in his gums. Suddenly, a spider skittered out of his mouth and down over his chin.

Joringel spun away from the dead man—tearing a long, beaded line of red across his nose and face. Joringel grimaced. But he told himself, "In the castle, no one feels any pain." And he pushed on.

He could see the wall now. The stones were heavy and gray and crusted with yellow lichen. As Joringel got closer, he slowed.

His shirt was soaked with sweat, and his breathing was heavy. He came to a stop. *I'll just rest here for a moment,* he thought. His eyelids drooped. *It would be so easy just to sleep . . .*

And then he noticed that someone was standing just where the thicket embraced the stone wall. Joringel shook himself. *No,* he thought. *Don't sleep yet.* And he forced his exhausted muscles to push on.

The body at the edge of the thicket was not a body. It was a skeleton. Shreds of clothes hung from its bones. A bird had made a nest in the man's rib cage.

That is disgusting.

Joringel followed the lichen-encrusted wall until he found an opening. He tore forward, the fingers of thorns gripping his clothes and skin and hair as if they would not let him go until, with a great gasp, he broke from the thicket and through the space in the wall.

Joringel found himself in a castle courtyard. It was much like a typical castle courtyard—there was a barracks festooned with shields in the eastern corner, a stream with a water wheel and laundry pots to the west, and so on—but littered around the courtyard were bodies sprawled upon the ground, as if they had been in the middle of doing whatever they normally did and then suddenly fallen down dead.

Joringel's knees knocked gently together as he made his way to the nearest body. It was dressed as a washerwoman, and sure enough, a mess of linens lay across the short green grass nearby, as if they'd been hurled to the turf when she collapsed. The washerwoman lay facedown. Joringel gingerly turned her over. He pulled back. She was a very old woman—much too old to be a washerwoman. Her mouth hung open, but her eyes were gently shut, and a line of spittle ran from her mouth to her chin. Joringel put his head by her face. He could feel the gentle pulse of breath.

"Hello? Wake up! Are you okay?" he shouted at her. But the old woman did not stir.

Joringel made his way through the yard, occasionally turning over another body to find another old person, dressed as someone much younger, and each fast asleep. Joringel was unable to wake any of them.

He pushed open the door to the kitchens. There, he saw a man—not ancient, as most of the others had been, but clearly into middle age—half naked on the ground. He wore the tatters of what appeared to be children's clothes. Spattered around him on the floor were shattered eggs, their yolks brown and rock hard. Behind the man in boy's clothing, a shriveled crone lay in a puddle of apron and frock, as if clad in the garb of a fat woman.

Joringel picked his way through the kitchens, careful not to tread on anyone. He climbed narrow stairs into a great hall. Here, a banquet had been laid out. Two dozen people seemed to have done face-plants in their soup. Joringel climbed a broad staircase away from the hall.

He walked through deserted corridors and peeked into rooms where ancient lords and ladies lay in heaps on the rich rugs. All the windows were shrouded with brambles.

Finally, Joringel found a narrow stair where the windows were bright and airy. The thicket had not yet grown tall enough to cover these, for they led to the great tower that brooded over the valley. Joringel climbed up and up and up until he found himself in a small room. In the center of the room stood a bed, richly hung with bright fabrics. In the bed lay a girl. A beautiful girl. Unlike the others, she did not appear to be sleeping. She appeared to be dead.

Joringel approached her. He bent over her. Her delicate eyelids were closed. Her red lips were barely parted. Her locks,

ADAM GIDWITZ

silky and dark, surrounded her face like a halo. Joringel drew his face closer to the girl's. Closer still. He thought he could feel breath, breaking ever so faintly, over her lips.

Joringel leaned over and . . .

Kissed her.

Right?

He kisses her, and she wakes up, and they get married. Everyone knows that. Even the Brothers Grimm tell us that.

Which is why everyone, including the Brothers Grimm, are wrong.

(Sure, you're thinking. The Brothers Grimm are wrong, and *you* are right? Why should we believe *you*? Well, maybe I'll explain it to you later. If you're nice.)

Anyway, what really happened was this:

Joringel leaned over and grabbed the girl by the shoulders and hauled her into a sitting position. Her head listed off to one side lifelessly. Joringel then tried to lift her to her feet, in the hope that no one could remain sleeping standing up. He had gotten her halfway to her feet when her legs gave out under her, he lost his grip, and she went crashing to the floor. Her hip hit the bare floorboards, and her head followed. Joringel did not move.

"*Oops*," he whispered.

Just then, the girl's body shook. It shook again. Then it heaved, and a horrible scratching sound came from her throat and then she coughed and coughed and then she threw up.

There, on the floor, lay a chunk of apple.

The girl sat back against the bed, breathing hard.

"Hi," said Joringel, staring at her. "Are you okay?"

She looked at him from the corner of her eye. She nodded.

"Oh," Joringel said. "Good." Then he said, "I'm Joringel."

The girl's heaving slowed. "I'm Briar Rose," she said. And then she said, "Why are you here?"

"I wanted to come to the castle where no one felt any pain." Joringel paused.

The girl watched him.

"But now I'm not sure I want to stay." He looked confused, and a little bit afraid.

"Why?" Briar Rose asked. "What's wrong?"

Joringel helped her to her feet and led her down the winding stairs from the tower. They passed through the eerily silent corridors and down to the grand hall. There, the dozen people had their faces buried in their bowls. Briar Rose's eyes went wide.

"What's wrong with them?" she demanded. She approached her mother and father, their faces submerged in a black mud that was once puree of carrot. She took her mother's head and lifted it. Briar Rose screamed. She let her mother's face fall back onto the table with a thud.

"She's a crone!" Briar Rose screamed. "What's wrong with her? Is she dead?" She moved cautiously to her father and lifted his face from the soup. She dropped him too, and his face shattered the soup bowl. "What's wrong with them all? They look so old!"

Joringel shrugged. "You tell me."

So Briar Rose told Joringel of the Wise Woman's curse, and her promise to make the pain go away.

"You've been asleep?"

"I guess so."

"For how long?"

Briar Rose examined her mother again. "It looks like forty years have passed." Her voice was distant and sad. "I think I've missed everything." A sob broke from her throat, and Briar Rose fell to the floor. Joringel knelt down beside her and let her rest her head on his shoulder as she cried.

As the sound of her sobs echoed through the halls of the dormant castle, the sleepers began to stir. Off in the stables, a horse shook its head and whinnied. The hounds stretched and whined and began to wag their tails. The pigeons on the roof took their heads out from under their wings. The fly on the wall began to crawl again. The fire in the kitchen flamed up and cooked the meal, the roast began to crackle, and then even the ancient cook, now too thin for her apron, got to her feet and yanked the now middle-aged kitchen boy's hair.

The people in the castle all stood and marveled at one another's wrinkles and tried to figure out what had happened.

And still Briar Rose wept on Joringel's shoulder. The little boy wondered at the magic that a few tears had wrought, as the girl muttered, "I missed it all . . ."

Within a few hours, the brambles around the castle had withered back into the ground, and the castle was surrounded with a field of purple flowers. And Joringel took his leave of Briar Rose and her ancient, astounded parents.

As he walked through the violet field, picking his way past the corpses of princes in various stages of decomposition, the wind blowing the pollen sweet and thick into his hair, Joringel imagined that every flower was a weed. He stomped on them furiously. But the pain, and fear, and anger would not go away.

Where is Jorinda? he wondered. He missed her. He didn't want to. He was furious at her for leaving him. Thinking about her, or his mother, or anything from home, caused sharp shooting pains in his head. He tried to stamp down the feelings like so many flowers in a field.

But it didn't help. Not at all. There were millions and millions of flowers.

The
Black Foal

Once upon a time, a girl walked, aimless and lonely, through the rich, green wood behind the Castle Grimm. The leaves glowed golden in the warm sun, and birds seemed to be playing a game of tag out in front of the girl's path.

But the beautiful wood did not cheer Jorinda.

She came to a clearing where there stood a great oak tree. Bunches of acorns hung from its gnarled boughs. A squirrel shimmying up its trunk stopped and watched Jorinda suspiciously, and then disappeared around the far side of the tree.

Jorinda put her back against the oak's rough bark and slid down until her rear rested on the warm, damp ground. She sighed.

Joringel was gone. She had sent people to look for him. There was no trace. He had been at home one day, and the next, he wasn't. It was her fault. Jorinda closed her eyes. Tears poked at the backs of her lids. She tried to choke them off. *Push it down*, she told herself. *Don't cry.*

But tears are sneaky. One crawled between her tightly shut lashes and began wending its way toward Jorinda's chin.

Back in the castle, the king sat gloomily on his throne. Plush cloth hung from the ceilings. Wide windows gave out onto the thick, green Kingswood.

The prince sat on a velvet step at the king's feet. "I don't know what I saw in her," he sighed.

"Well," the king responded, pulling at his beard, "she's clever. And she's brave. But you're not terribly interested in those qualities. Are you?"

"Not really. She did look nice in that red dress."

"Yes! Always a good criterion for choosing a bride. How she looks in a red dress."

The prince, who did not do well with sarcasm, perked up, "Yeah! That's what I thought!"

The king tugged at his beard. "What is to be done? You cannot marry a child. Nor a servant. Not even a servant as brave and clever as Jorinda." He cursed. "She survived Malchizedek! How? She must be able to do anything!"

"Anything?" The prince looked up at his father.

"Well, practically."

"Can she say the alphabet backward?"

The king squinted at his son. "I don't know. Maybe."

"Wow," murmured the prince. Then he said, "Can she do this?" And he curled up his tongue into a little tube.

"I'm not sure, son," the king sighed.

"I bet she can't," the prince said, satisfied with himself. And then he stopped. "Can she ride a unicorn? I would love to ride a unicorn. . . ."

"Boy, unicorns aren't real. You know that. I've told you that. A number of times."

"Oh. Right." The prince looked crestfallen. "I would like to ride a unicorn."

Just then, the door opened a crack, and in slipped a short, stocky man with a grizzled beard. He wore leather breeches and a leather jerkin and a leather patch over one eye.

"Ah! Fänger!" the king exclaimed, brightening at the sight of his capable master of the hunt. "Come in!" The huntsman approached, his footfall soundless even on the stone floor. The king lowered his voice. "I need your help. It seems that my son here was a little *rash* in his choice of a bride."

"Ah. I see."

"Something needs to happen to her."

Fänger nodded.

"An accident," the king said.

The prince looked up. "Like, in her pants?"

The king exhaled loudly.

Fänger said, "You can rely on me, your highness." The huntsman bowed to the king and the prince and slipped silently from the room.

"What kind of accident?" the prince asked. "Number one or number two?"

The king closed his eyes and rubbed his temples.

Jorinda had fallen asleep in the warm sun. In her dreams, she was riding away from Joringel on the prince's horse. She looked back to see him, but he wasn't there. He was in their mother's study. She knew that, somehow. She ached to be with them. But the horse wouldn't turn around. It galloped down the hot roads, and her cheek rubbed against the prince's rough shirt. She could really feel it—the coarse, warm fabric scratching her cheek.

Her eyes flew open. She nearly screamed.

There was a horse licking her face.

It was barely a horse. It was small and delicate, with spindly legs and a small, round trunk. It was a foal, as black as midnight.

She had startled the little foal. He had pulled back and was staring with wide eyes.

Which made Jorinda laugh.

The foal watched her for a moment, uncertain. Then, slowly, he came toward her again and resumed licking her face.

She laughed again.

He pulled back, watching her. Then he hopped to the left and pawed the ground.

"What do you want?" Jorinda smiled.

He hopped to the right and pawed the ground again.

"What are you doing?"

Then he sneezed. Jorinda laughed loudly. The little horse shook his black head and approached the girl a third time. Very slowly, he folded his too-thin legs underneath himself, lay down, and put his head in her lap.

Jorinda began to stroke the foal's jet black mane. It was like silk. She ran her thin fingers up to his forehead, brushing the short, thick hair of his hide with her fingernails. And there, on his forehead, she felt a bump. More than a bump, really. A small stump, made of smooth horn that twisted like a braid. It was very small. No more than an inch long.

The little girl looked at the foal with his head in her lap. Her eyes narrowed. The corners of her mouth turned up as she whispered, "What, exactly, are you?"

Day after day, Jorinda came to the clearing in the Kingswood and sat beneath the great oak tree. She brought the little foal carrots and apples and other treats, and he sniffed at them with his unbelievably soft nose and ate them right from her hand. Once he had eaten, he'd bound around the clearing, trying to get her to play with him. Sometimes she did, jumping up and chasing him here and there. She could never catch him—his little hooves could change direction in an instant—but he would taunt her, pawing the ground and hopping from side to side. And then Jorinda would get tired, and collapse under the oak tree. And he would hop from side to side again, hoping to provoke her into chasing him some more. But she would only laugh. So he would sneeze and shake his head, and she would laugh harder. And then he would fold up his spindly little legs and lower his head into her lap. Often they slept through the hot, sunny afternoons under the great oak tree just like that.

One evening, as dusk fell, Jorinda opened her eyes. The little foal was still asleep in her lap. She sighed. "If you never leave me, little horse, I will never leave you."

The foal opened his eyes and sneezed.

"Okay." Jorinda giggled. "So we agree."

The walls of the royal hunting lodge were lined with the skulls of deer. Seven hundred and three skulls, to be exact. Fänger didn't have to count them. He knew. A pity he wouldn't be able to put the skull of his latest victim on the wall. Wouldn't be proper.

The deers' antlers spread like dead, blanched trees from white bone. In the flickering candlelight of the early, early morning, their shadows looked like great spiderwebs clinging to the walls.

Fänger fletched the final arrow for his quiver and picked up his longbow. There were not ten men in the whole kingdom who could pull his bow. An arrow loosed from it would go straight through a man. Fänger knew. He had tried it.

He dropped his hatchet through a loop on his belt. The hatchet was for cleanup work. If he was out hunting with the king and the king missed his shot (as he often did), Fänger would go follow the dogs, springing over hedges and under hemlocks, and fall upon the poor, flailing beast. And with one swift blow, the hatchet would fall and the spine would be severed and the beast would lie still.

Fänger slipped out the door in the cool, early morning.

It was before dawn. The moon hung low in the sky, and the stars up above glittered dimly. The dew speckled the huntsman's boots as he made his way to a low hedge, just a stone's throw from the door to the royal chambers. He crouched behind it and waited.

He could have done it in Jorinda's bed, as the little girl slept. Even if she slept lightly, he could have buried the hatchet in her skull before the scream left her lips. But Fänger was a hunter. And he preferred to hunt.

Okay. Maybe you feel a little worried right now. Maybe you're not sure you want to read a story about a little girl being *hunted*.

I find that hard to believe, frankly. You seemed to have no trouble reading a story about a little boy being decapitated, or two young women dismembering themselves, or a little girl being strangled by a corpse . . .

But perhaps you've just about reached your breaking point, and you can't take any more.

Or perhaps it is not the little girl you're worried about. Perhaps it's the little black horse. Perhaps you are worried about what will happen to him.

Yeah, I can't blame you.

ADAM GIDWITZ

Jorinda rolled over lazily as the sun broke through her window. Someone was chopping wood down in the courtyard. She put a pillow over her head. Her blankets tumbled off her and fell to the floor.

She dressed quickly, walked through the kitchens—grabbing two apples from a wooden bowl as she went—and hurried out the door to the Kingswood. She ran past a low hedge, past the kennels where hunting dogs yowled and snarled at one another, past the hunting lodge with its hundreds of skulls, and into the forest. She did not notice that a figure was following her at a distance.

She arrived at the clearing and sat with her back to the oak. She did not notice the figure peering at her from behind a nearby hemlock.

She began to eat one of the apples, while the other sat in her lap. She did not notice the figure silently draw an arrow from his quiver and place it, ever so quietly, on his bowstring.

She did not notice him pull the string back, bending the heavy bow as few men could, and raise the arrow to his good eye.

She did not notice him breathe out nice and slow.

Nor did she notice his one eye grow wider, and his bowstring go slack, and his bow drop silently, limply, to his side.

For her little friend had appeared beside her, and he was nuzzling her neck with a nose so soft it defied belief. She giggled as he tried to chew on her hair. She gave him his apple. He ate it in three bites, core and all. Then he began to leap friskily from side to side and paw the ground, asking Jorinda to play their favorite game.

As the western sky turned red and gold, and the east became a royal blue dappled with gray spools of wool, the little girl stood up from her afternoon nap, stretched her arms high, and sighed. The little foal sneezed softly, and Jorinda kissed him on the nose. She walked to the edge of the little clearing and turned back. He was watching her every move. She smiled at him, waved, and began to make her way back to the castle.

The figure crouching behind the hemlock stayed where he was. He watched the little black beast sneeze once more, shake his midnight head, paw the ground, and then turn and disappear into the wood.

Fänger fingered the razor edge of his hatchet, shook his head, and smiled.

——

"She is not dead."

"No, sire."

The king put his chin on his folded hands and looked out from under heavy brows. "I was pretty sure she wasn't dead when she came into the hall for dinner this evening."

"Yes, sire."

"And when she finished her cauliflower soup, and her bratwurst, and all her sauerkraut, I was even further convinced."

"Yes, sire."

"And when she ate every bit of her black chocolate cake, I came to the unimpeachable conclusion that she is, indeed, NOT DEAD."

The huntsman bowed his head.

"So, Fänger, before I throw you in the stocks for mutiny and deception, I will give you one sentence to answer this question." And then the king shouted, "WHY NOT?"

Fänger took a deep breath. "There was a unicorn, sir."

The king opened his lips to respond, and then he closed them again. Over in a corner, the prince looked up from his stack of colored blocks. (He had had them since he was a child; he still found stacking them a pleasant challenge.)

"Okay," said the king. "One more sentence."

"I followed her into the forest and was about to pierce her

little heart with an arrow, when a unicorn approached and put his head in her lap."

The king was staring now, and his mouth was not entirely closed.

"May I have another sentence, your highness?"

The king nodded dumbly.

"It is a juvenile. A foal. It has a very small horn. But it is, without any doubt, a unicorn."

The prince shouted, "I want to ride it!"

His father cringed. "Fänger, that horn . . ."

"Priceless, sire. Utterly without measure."

"I can kill the beast myself?"

Fänger inclined his head.

"You have a plan?"

"Of course, sire."

"And the girl?"

"After, your majesty."

The king smiled and rubbed his hands together. "Excellent, Fänger! Oh, this is excellent!"

"Wait!" the prince exclaimed. "After you kill it, can I ride it?"

The king looked at his son like he had two heads. "Um . . . sure."

"Good," the prince sighed. "I've always wanted to ride a unicorn."

Every day that week, the huntsman followed Jorinda out of the palace, through the wood, and to her spot under the great oak tree. And on the sixth day, after she and her little friend had parted, the huntsman set to making a great blind.

A "blind," in case you don't know, is where a hunter waits for his quarry.

"Quarry," in case you don't know, is what you call the animal that the hunter is trying to kill.

If you don't know what "animal" or "trying" or "kill" means, this book is probably above your reading level.

On the seventh day, no one followed the little girl into the Kingswood. No one needed to. Because they already knew where she was going. And they were already there, waiting for her.

She didn't see them, though. Fänger was an expert at building blinds. And besides, Jorinda was too excited. She had brought sugar cubes. She had never fed her little friend sugar cubes before. But she was pretty sure he would love them.

Jorinda ran on her toes, flying through the underbrush to the clearing. She sat down beneath the great oak and spread out her little skirt over her knees and held the sugar cubes tightly in her hand.

She waited.

And waited.

And waited.

Behind the blind of branches, the king sat on his horse. An arrow lay in his palm. His bow dangled from his saddle. He huffed impatiently. Fänger, standing at the king's side, put his finger to his lips. The king rolled his eyes and looked back to the clearing.

Jorinda began to worry. Where was her little friend? Would he not come? Had something happened to him?

In the blind, Fänger ran his thumb over the blade of his hatchet. A red line rose to the surface of his skin. The blade was sharp enough. He sucked away the blood.

And just then, from the opposite brush, a small creature emerged. Its legs were uncertain and spindly. Its coat was shimmering like a lake in the moonlight. Its mane hung lank and soft as silk across its neck. And on its forehead, protruding just an inch or so, was an ebony horn.

The king gasped.

The small beast approached Jorinda. His soft nose sniffed first at her open hand—at her palm, her wrist, her fingers. He sneezed. She laughed. Then he moved over to her closed hand, the one that held the sugar cubes.

Fänger nodded to the king. The king nocked an arrow in his bow, pulled the string back, and raised the arrow to his face. Fänger hefted his hatchet.

The unicorn had eaten the sugar cubes. Now he was licking the residue from Jorinda's hand, her wrist, her arm. She laughed as he snuffled up to her neck, her face. "Stop!" she giggled, pushing his head away. "Stop!"

But then she stopped. For in the reflection of the beast's round eye she saw a man astride a horse, a bow and arrow drawn and aimed, emerging from behind a wall of leaves.

She turned. The king's eyes were flashing, and his red face was twisted into a horrific smile.

"DON'T!" Jorinda screamed. And she threw her little body in front of the foal's neck at the very instant the king loosed his arrow.

Everything was moving very slowly. Jorinda saw the arrow wobble for a moment as it left the bow, and then the feathers caught the wind, it found its course, and it sailed, straight and true, for the unicorn and the little girl.

At first, it just burned. A dull burn below Jorinda's neck. She looked to see what made her feel that way.

Then she saw the blood spattered on the black coat of the unicorn, and the arrow spinning wildly away from them through the air.

She looked at the little beast. The blood made a pattern on its side. She thought it looked like a juniper tree. *Where is the wound?* she wondered.

And then the pain lanced through her, and she screamed, and her arms squeezed the unicorn's neck, and then she was on his back, and they were off.

The little unicorn careered through the wood, leaping logs and bushes and branches without an instant's hesitation. Jorinda held on to his neck and his mane for dear life, as her blood flowed down his side, spraying the leaves as they galloped past.

The king's horse was not far behind. They could hear the man cursing his missed shot and bellowing for Fänger to keep up. The king's horse was larger than the little unicorn, and so less nimble. But its great legs pounded the bracken underfoot, and what time it lost by going around the shrubs it made up with its huge strides. The king spurred his horse mercilessly and held his bow tight.

Not far behind him, Fänger wove and ducked through the trees. And while he had not the agility of the little unicorn, nor

ADAM GIDWITZ

the raw speed of the great horse, he was crafty and knew these woods well. He often fell behind, only to take a shortcut down an escarpment or through the thickest brush and arrive again just behind the chase.

And so it happened that Fänger lost sight of the king's horse, but saw the blood on the leaves, guessed where the unicorn was going, and turned aside. He ran as fast as he could, unhooking his hatchet from his belt, ducking under branches and leaping beds of ivy, until he came to a steep hill. He slid down the hill on his side, ripping up the roots and ferns as he fell, and came crashing to the ground in a clearing with a cliff on one side and the steep hill on the other. Standing at one end of the clearing was the little unicorn. The girl was draped over his back, her head against his neck, heaving raggedly. Both of them were covered in blood. At the other end of the clearing was the king. His arrow was nocked, his bow raised, his shoulders rising up and down, up and down.

"I got 'em!" the king said aloud, grinning. "I got 'em!" His eyes narrowed. He pulled the bowstring back.

"Run!" Jorinda screamed to the unicorn. But there was nowhere to go. The cliff was behind him, the steep hill to his side. He shook his long black head and pawed the ground.

"Run!" Jorinda was crying now. "Please! Run! They'll kill you!"

The king said, "I'll get the beast. Afterwards, Fänger, you get her."

"Please," the little girl wept. "Plea—"

She stopped. She stared at the king.

Or, perhaps, not at the king. Perhaps just behind the king.

Fänger followed her gaze. "SIRE!"

The king had just raised the bow to his face. The string was taut, the arrow ready. He heard his huntsman's cry. He released the arrow, but the shot was high and wide. He heard the sound of hoofbeats crashing through the wood behind him. He turned.

Fänger lifted his hatchet to hurl it.

Too late.

With the force of an explosion, the king was taken off his horse. A long black horn, smooth and twining and very, very sharp at the end, entered his back, passed through his spine, his lungs, and his heart, and emerged just under his chin.

Fänger gaped as another great black horn emerged from the forest. The thunder of hooves was deafening. He tried to change his hatchet's target, from the first beast to the second, but the creature was moving too fast. All Fänger could do was lift his arms to his face.

The black horn went straight through his chest. He was driven backward, into the side of the steep hill, and the horn went so far through him that it stuck into the stony black earth.

The two adult unicorns withdrew their horns from the

corpses of the two men. Then they pranced around the clearing, shaking their heads, either searching for more enemies or warning others off. At last, they approached their little foal. Jorinda slid to the ground, smearing blood across his black, glistening flanks.

The foal trotted to the adults and bowed his head, and they came up alongside him and nestled their muzzles in his neck. After a moment, the little unicorn extricated himself from the equine embrace and approached Jorinda. He put his soft nose next to her cheek. She closed her eyes.

When she opened her eyes again, she saw the three unicorns disappearing into the forest.

Jorinda stood in the center of the corpse-strewn, blood-drenched clearing. Blood flowed swiftly from her shoulder. Tears cut lines down her filthy cheeks.

And the only thought she had was, *Even unicorns have parents.*

Then she fell to her knees and wept.

Everyone okay out there?

Are you sure?

'Cause I'm just barely hanging on myself. . . .

Okay?

You sure?

All right.

Here we go.

The
Ivory Monkey

Once upon a time, a boy wandered through distant lands. He traversed dark forests, he scaled enormous mountains, he waded through spring-swollen rivers, he sat on great rocks overlooking the sea.

Something was not right. He felt ill. All the time. Like he was carrying a small lake inside his stomach.

Over his shoulder, the three ravens flew. Sometimes they tried to engage him in conversation. Other times, they let him sulk.

But one day, as Joringel pushed through the heavy brush of a red and yellow wood, the ravens became excited.

"Hey!" cried the second, coming to perch on a gnarly branch. "Do you know where we are?"

"We know everything," answered the third, gliding down beside him.

"It's sort of what we *do*," added the first, landing beside his brothers.

"Well?" smiled the second. "Where?"

The first raven put his beak into the air. "49.173 longitude, 9.435 latitude."

Joringel kept walking. He was used to them saying things that made absolutely no sense.

"Which means . . . ?" The second raven led them on, expectantly.

"We're near a McDonald's?" the third said.

"Yeah, not for another seven hundred years," scowled the second raven. "Come on! You're not trying."

The first raven furrowed his black brow. "49.173, 9.435 . . . north of the Crystal Mountain . . . south of the kingdom of Märchen . . . west of the Schwarzwald . . ."

"THE MONKEY!" the third raven screamed.

The second raven broke into a wide grin. (I have no idea what a raven grinning looks like. You'll have to try to picture that yourself.) "The monkey!"

The first raven's eyes lit up. "The monkey!"

"THE MONKEY!!!!!!!" the third raven howled. Then he did a little dance on the branch of the tree.

The second raven swooped down into Joringel's path. "Come this way," he instructed him. "We have something we want to show you."

Joringel had been wrestling ferociously with the sickness in his stomach. When he spoke, he tasted bile. "What is it?"

The second raven sang, "You'll like it . . ."

The first swooped down and sat on Joringel's head. "We promise!"

"Get off!" the little boy snapped, waving his arms at the raven. The first raven leaped up into the air and then landed on his head again. "Come on, grumpy! Let's go!"

The third raven was already flying off into the trees, roaring, "THE MONKEY!!!!!!!!!!!!!!!!!!!!"

Joringel followed the three ravens through the thick foliage, all red and yellow and orange in the cool autumn air. Fallen leaves lay wet and slick over the earth, and the pop of branches under his feet was muted, soft, from recent rain.

Joringel grumbled to himself, fought with whatever was pushing up from the bottom of his stomach, and emerged into a clearing. His breath caught.

In the center of the clearing was a statue. It was of a beautiful young person—made of smooth marble. Its face was calm and clear and was neither boy nor girl. Its eyes reminded

Joringel of his sister. But Joringel knew it would have reminded you of anyone you missed. It was that kind of statue. His heart hurt.

The statue's arm was outstretched. In its extended hand sat a little monkey, carved from ivory.

Joringel approached it.

The white monkey sat on its haunches, and its round eyes peered up at Joringel as if it might speak at any moment. It was the most lifelike, adorable carving of a monkey Joringel had ever seen.

"Cute, isn't it?" said the first raven, landing on the statue's head.

Joringel nodded.

"It is very powerful," said the second raven, landing on the statue's shoulder.

The third raven landed right on the statue's outstretched arm, no more than a foot away from the little monkey. "Well?" he asked. "What do you see?"

Joringel glanced up at him, and then back to the monkey. "What do you mean?"

The third raven said, "Just tell me what you see."

"Uh . . ." said Joringel. "I see a monkey?"

"Go on," said the third raven.

"An ivory monkey?"

"Yes . . . ?"

"A cute ivory monkey?"

And as soon as Joringel had said it, his eyes grew wide, he went stiff as a board, and he tumbled like a felled tree to the ground.

"YES!" shrieked the third raven.

"Works every time!" crowed the second.

"Never gets old!" chuckled the first.

The third raven continued to shriek, "I LOVE THE MONKEY!!!!!!"

After a few minutes, Joringel came to. He sat up, rubbed his head, and said, "What happened?"

The third raven was singing, "The monkey go-o-ot you! You didn't kno-o-ow it! But then it g-o-ot you! 'Cause it's so aw-w-wesome!"

Joringel was blinking. "What?"

"You fell under the power of the monkey," the first raven explained.

"I did?"

"Don't you feel it?" asked the second.

"My head hurts," Joringel replied.

"Stand up," the first raven instructed him.

Joringel pulled himself to his feet.

"Jump up and down," the second raven said.

Joringel began to jump up and down.

"Slap yourself in the face!" the third raven shouted.

Joringel continued to jump up and down while he slapped himself in the face.

"I LOVE THE MONKEY!!!!!!!" the third raven shrieked.

"Say, 'cute ivory monkey' again," the first raven commanded.

"Cute ivory monkey again," replied Joringel.

The first raven muttered, "Close enough."

Joringel suddenly stopped jumping up and down and slapping himself in the face.

"Hey!" Joringel cried. "Wow!"

"Now do you understand the power of the monkey?" asked the second raven.

"If I'm holding the monkey, or touching this statue," explained the first, "and you say 'cute ivory monkey,' you will fall under my control."

Joringel squinted at the first raven. "But you just said it."

"I know, but I'm touching the statue. So it has no effect on me. Likewise if you were holding the monkey."

"Huh," said Joringel. He looked up at the ravens. "Can I take it?"

"No!" cried the first raven.

"Absolutely not!" gasped the second.

"Under no circumstances!" shrieked the third.

"Why not?" Joringel asked.

The three ravens looked at one another. Silently, they decided that the first raven should explain it.

"This stone is cursed," he began. "For while, it is a funny trick—"

"Hilarious!" the third raven shouted.

"It is not to be taken from this grove," the first went on. "The greatest misfortune will befall whoever takes it from here."

The three ravens fell into an ominous silence.

But Joringel was not in the mood to be impressed. "Greater misfortune than having your head cut off?"

The three ravens looked at one another.

"Or being eaten by your mother?"

"*You remember that?*" the first raven whispered. "We thought you didn't remember—"

"Or turning into a bird?"

"Hey! What's so bad about being a bird?" the second raven objected.

"Or having your sister abandon you? Or playing with corpses? Or wandering for weeks and weeks with no one to talk to except some ravens who can see the future?"

"Are we really that bad?" the third asked, trying not to let on that Joringel had hurt his feelings.

Joringel didn't care. Whatever was sloshing around his stomach and pushing at his eyes and twining around his throat like an out-of-control weed was winning, and he didn't care anymore. He grabbed the ivory monkey from its perch on the statue's outstretched hand and stormed from the clearing without another word.

The three ravens stared after him.

Suddenly, the third shrieked, "THE MONKEY!!!!!!!!"

But the second just sighed.

And the first said, "Let him go. After all, he'll need it."

"He'll need a lot more than that," the second added.

But the third just said, "The monkey . . ."

The Tyrants

Once upon a time, a little girl walked past two mangled corpses, through a great wood, tracing the path of blood and broken branches back to the great oak laden with acorns. She wound her way out of the forest, past the hunting lodge—empty now, save for the skulls—past the kennels, past the hedge.

She entered the castle's kitchens. A cook caught sight of her and screamed.

The little girl collapsed in a bloody heap.

When Jorinda awoke, two days later, all of the king's most important courtiers were gathered around her bedside. Their long, gray faces hovered over her, their cracked lips hanging open.

"What?" demanded the little girl.

The courtiers gasped.

"She lives!"

"It's a miracle!"

"A blessed miracle!"

Jorinda blinked and wiped the crust from her mouth.

"And?" asked the senior courtier, who had the longest and grayest face of the lot. "Where is the king?"

"Dead," Jorinda replied. "The huntsman, too."

The room fell deathly still.

"How?" the courtier asked.

Jorinda opened her mouth—and then she closed it again. Unicorns? Either they wouldn't believe her, or they would set out to hunt them. Likely both. So instead, she responded, "We were attacked. I don't know by whom."

The courtiers gasped. Attacked? In the Kingswood? "Could you see what the assailants looked like? What they were wearing?"

Jorinda thought. "They were covered in black. They had long spears. And they rode horses."

The senior courtier straightened his back and stared into the distance. "Assassins," he muttered. "This is grave. Very grave indeed."

"We must consider our options."

"We must consult with the prince."

"Well . . . perhaps we'll consider our options before we consult with the prince."

"Right. Good thinking."

And the courtiers fled the room in a storm of voices.

Jorinda put her head back on the pillow and closed her eyes.

Late that night, the door to her room opened, and four serving women bustled in. They carried a candelabra, and in the arms of one lay a long white dress.

Jorinda sat up. "What's that for?"

"What do you think? Your wedding!"

"What? When?"

"When? Child, didn't they tell you?"

"No," Jorinda said, narrowing her eyes. "When am I to be married?"

"In half an hour!"

The wedding was a hurried affair. The courtiers all stood for the duration of the ceremony, and the bishop read from his Bible so quickly that Jorinda couldn't understand what she was vowing and swearing and assenting to. The prince's knees were knocking together through the whole ritual. Jorinda didn't know what was going on.

But at the end of the ceremony, the handsome and clever prince bent over, kissed Jorinda on the cheek, and said, "Goodbye. And good luck." And then he was swept from the room.

"Where is he going?" Jorinda demanded.

The senior courtier approached her. "He's fleeing the kingdom, of course. If there are assassins about, it isn't safe for him to stay here."

Jorinda cocked her head. "But I'm staying?"

"Someone has to sit on the throne!" the courtier exclaimed. And then he dashed from the room after the prince.

And so it was that Jorinda became the queen of the Kingdom of Grimm.

Let me say right now that none of the tales of the Brothers Grimm tell of this period in the kingdom's history. Go through that musty old book that sits in the corner of your library. You won't read about a single kingdom ruled by a little girl.

But ruled by her it was.

Now, you might expect, with a little girl on the throne, that instead of having to pay taxes, people would be given lollipops, and that instead of an army, the kingdom would just have a bunch of pillow fights and hair-braiding sessions.

You might expect that. But then, you would expect wrong.

The stories do not talk of the reign of Queen Jorinda because she was a tyrant. A tyrant, in case you're unfamiliar with the word, is a terrible and cruel leader who doesn't respect any laws but his or her own. It comes from the same word as *Tyrannosaurus*. Which should tell you something.

So Queen Ashputtle was a tyrant. A tyrant no taller than a man's belly button, it is true. But a tyrant nonetheless.

Why, you are asking, was Jorinda a tyrant?

Allow me to explain.

For the first few weeks of Jorinda's rule, everything was all right. She was given a tour of the palace, she was schooled in the ways of governance, she met with representatives of the kingdom's allies and enemies, and everyone thought she managed herself rather well.

But inside, she was not doing so well at all. Something was sloshing away inside of Jorinda. Every time someone bowed to her, she felt it, churning in her achy stomach. Every time a subject waved and smiled, it stabbed at the bottom of her mind. Every time a visiting dignitary told her how brave or impressive she was, it twined itself around her lungs and took her breath away.

Worst of all was at night. At night, thoughts of her mother's closed study door, and of a great iron stew pot, and of her brother standing and watching her ride away rose before her whenever she closed her eyes.

Don't feel it, Jorinda told herself. *Smother it down, choke it back, stamp it out.*

So whenever someone bowed to her, she frowned and pushed her feelings down. And whenever a subject waved and smiled, she jerked her head away so as not to see, not to feel. And whenever anyone complimented her at all, she sneered at herself, and at them, and fought, fought, fought the pain within.

Well, feelings become words, and words become deeds, and over time, Jorinda was not only sneering at compliments, but also at complaints. She was not only jerking her head away to avoid seeing smiles, but also to avoid seeing tears. She frowned not just at those who bowed to her. She frowned at everyone.

She had her courtiers bring her a dozen mattresses, and then a dozen more. She slept on twenty-five of them, teetering forty feet in the air. But no matter how many mattresses she slept on, she tossed and turned in agony.

Jorinda was fighting something on the inside. And whatever is inside does not stay inside for long.

———

As the little girl monarch became colder and crueler, rumors began to swirl, sweeping through the kingdom like a winter dust storm.

Queen Jorinda is not what she appears to be, they said. Not a sweet girl at all, but a monster! A usurper! A tyrant! She killed the king and his huntsman! How? Magic! Sorcery! A deal with the Devil!

But the prince would return, they whispered. He had fled, fearing the little girl and her unholy assassins. He would return, with an army at his back, and depose the little tyrant and retake his place on the throne!

Well, the rumor was poppycock, of course. Jorinda hadn't killed the king and his huntsman. The unicorns had. But rumors tend to take on a life of their own.

Have you ever heard of a "self-fulfilling prophecy"? That's like when someone says you'll fail a test, so you get so nervous you can't study, and then you actually *do* fail the test. The prophecy makes itself come true.

Well, rumors can be like that as well.

For Jorinda heard the rumors about the prince (he was actually the king now, or the king-in-hiding, or something like that—but I'm just going to keep calling him the prince, because I get confused easily). She had heard the rumors that he was trying to raise an army out in the wilderness, or perhaps allying himself with some neighboring king, who would then march upon Grimm and conquer it. It was just a rumor, but she believed it. Perhaps the prince did think that she had killed his father. And if he wanted to take his revenge, he would certainly have help. For who would fear a kingdom ruled by a little girl? He and some ally would try to conquer the kingdom, depose Jorinda, and then dispose of her. She was certain of it.

So she forced every man and boy above the age of sixteen to join her army. It soon became the largest army in the history of the kingdom. The soldiers spent every morning from dawn until noon marching up and down the dusty roads of Grimm, performing military drills in the fields that they should have been farming, and barking out chants like, "Who is the fiercest in the land? Jorinda of the iron hand!"

Now, maybe you know it, and maybe you don't, but outfitting an army of that size costs a fortune. So Jorinda wrung the money out of her poor citizens with crushing taxes. (She spared Malchizedek, though. To him, she kept all her promises.

Because it's best not to cross an ogre. And besides, she kind of liked him.) But the people starved in the dirt lanes as the tax collectors carted off half of all the produce of their fields, their mills, their workshops, their calloused and tired hands.

Jorinda had one captain whom she trusted above all the others. He was the cousin of the unfortunate Fänger, but he seemed to hold no grudge against the queen for the demise of his kinsman. Indeed, he seemed to feel nothing at all. His name was Herzlos. He had long black hair and deep scars that ran down his face like ancient riverbeds. Captain Herzlos was always happy to whip a shirking soldier or set fire to the house of a subject who would not pay his taxes. Whatever Jorinda's other captains shrank from, Herzlos would do. And with relish.

Six months went by, and then six months more. The shadow of the queen hung heavy over the entire kingdom. Soldiers marched in mindless unison, chanting of Jorinda's iron hand at the tops of their lungs, tramping over the once fertile fields until the crops were stomped into submission and the poor were starving to death in the narrow, dusty streets.

The age was, indeed, a grim one.

———

I know what you're thinking. You're thinking, How, how could Jorinda do all this? She seemed like such a nice girl!

Well, she was.

But even nice girls sometimes fight wars with themselves.

It was about a year after Jorinda had become Queen Jorinda, or Jorinda the Tyrant, that a visitor arrived at the castle's gates.

"I'm here to see the queen," he told the guards.

They scoffed. "No one sees the queen."

The visitor's mouth was set in a hard line. He stared up at the guards with dark eyes from under a curly mop of hair. "Send her a message. She will see me. If she doesn't, you can throw me in prison."

The guards smirked at one another. One replied, "We don't have prisons anymore. Just gallows."

"Fine," said the visitor. "If she doesn't want to see me after you give her my message, you can send me to the gallows to be hanged until I am dead."

More smirking. "All right, then. What's this message of yours?"

The visitor spoke very crisply: "If you won't leave me, I won't leave you."

Five minutes later, Joringel was being led through the dark halls of the Castle Grimm. As he passed grand staircases decked with great tapestries of gray and black, his stomach tossed and churned.

Choke it back, he thought. Just as he managed to wrestle the sickness in his stomach into submission, the guard led him into the throne room.

There she was. A little girl, regal and serene, on a great throne, with a towering, ornate crown on her head. Joringel felt something yank at his insides, as if he'd swallowed a fishhook. He looked at his sister.

Her lips had started to crinkle. Her eyes, he thought, were shining.

Joringel began to smile. For the first time in a long time.

Across the room, Jorinda felt something yank at her insides, too.

She saw her brother, and his lips were crinkling. His eyes shone.

Jorinda began to smile. For the first time in a long time.

But at exactly the moment that both children began to smile, their stomachs roared. A wave—a brown, dirty, tidal wave of feelings—crashed over them. They tried to stand firm. They tried to hold on. Jorinda forced the corners of her mouth back down. Joringel blinked hard to quell the tears. *Choke it back*, they both thought. *Smother it. Stamp it out.*

For a moment, neither moved.

And then, the tidal wave passed, and it took along with it everything they felt—all their happiness, all their sadness, all their anger, all their guilt—and left them as if marooned on a barren peninsula, wrecked by storm.

They approached one another.

Jorinda said, "Welcome, brother."

And Joringel replied, "Thank you, sister."

And they shook hands. Lest the storm rise again.

Joringel moved into a chamber in the castle not far from his sister. He stood beside her in the throne room when she made her decrees, and he went with her on her tours of the kingdom. He was restless, though, as he had little else to do. He had tried to help Herzlos manage the army. He soon gave it up, though. Joringel, it turned out, was a little frightened of Herzlos.

But one day, as the royal carriage rattled over the stony streets of Grimm's largest town, Joringel caught sight of a mother walking with her son. The woman's arms were laden with three sacks of potatoes, while the little boy behind her was struggling with one. "Don't you drop any of those," she told him.

"Okay, Mommy," the boy replied. He was teetering this way and that, trying to keep the sack from tumbling from his arms. But then the boy caught sight of the royal carriage. "Ooh, Mommy, look! The queen!" he said. And, because he was a little boy, he pointed at the carriage. Well, as soon as he did, the sack toppled over, and the potatoes went rolling into the street.

"Boy!" the woman bellowed, and, letting her potatoes drop to the ground as well, she spun and slapped her son across the face.

Before he knew what he was doing, Joringel was out of the carriage, leaping over potatoes, and grabbing the woman's arm. The woman turned to him, surprised. Which is when Joringel slapped her across the face, just as she had her son. And then he did it again. And once more.

The boy began to cry. The woman cowered.

"It is a new law," Joringel announced, "that any adult who harms a child shall be punished by the queen's soldiers threefold."

Joringel turned to see his sister, standing in the carriage. Her face was stone. "It is so decreed," was all she said.

Joringel turned back to the mother. He got very close to her face. "Never again," he said. "Never, ever again."

As the carriage rattled over the stony streets of Grimm, Joringel could hear the boy wailing. He tried to block it out and stamp down his roaring anger.

Joringel had found his role. While Jorinda dealt with questions of war and taxes, Joringel roamed the streets, followed by a group of the toughest soldiers—both women and men. As they roamed they kept an eye out for adults who were cruel to children. And when they found one they punished that adult bitterly.

And still the soldiers marched over the once-verdant fields, chanting, "Who's the strongest in the land? Jorinda of the iron hand!" So crops no longer grew in the Kingdom of Grimm. As soon as a tender green shoot dared to show itself above the ground, a soldier's boot stamped it into submission.

That year, gritty winter gave way to dusty summer without the pale green promise of spring.

Well? What do you think?

Should Joringel be punishing those parents like that?

And when did this book get so depressing?

And will it keep being this depressing?

I'm sorry. I know that no kid likes reading depressing books. I considered changing this part altogether. I considered not telling you the truth about what happened to these two children. About what they went through. And what it did to them. I considered telling you that Jorinda's reign really was all lollipops and pillow fights. And that Joringel was in charge of organizing huge games of capture the flag.

But I decided that I had to tell you the truth.

Because, you see, in life, every triumph begins with failure.

Don't worry, though. The triumph will come. We're almost there.

Jorinda sat straight up on top of her towering bed. Her sheets were sweaty and twisted. She could not catch her breath.

She shook herself. Just a nightmare. But it was terrible. She had been standing outside her mother's study. The door was locked. And her mother had been trying to get out, banging on the door. Banging. Banging.

BANG.

Jorinda jumped a foot. Shaking away her grogginess, she threw the covers off her great bed, climbed down the tall ladder her servants had constructed for her, and hurried to the chamber door.

She heard someone run by, whispering frantically.

BANG.

She opened the door an inch. A servant, carrying a candelabra, sprinted past, the candles flickering as she went.

BANG.

The floor was shaking.

Jorinda closed the door, locked it, and ran to the window. It was a grand window, for she lived in the royal chambers now. The window looked out over stone walls and down the great road that led to the Castle Grimm.

A pit opened up in Jorinda's stomach.

The road was lit by a thousand torches. And it was teeming. With men on horseback. With shouting peasants. And soldiers. Thousands of soldiers.

BANG.

Jorinda screamed. Just outside of the window, she saw a face. She fell back into the room.

"Open the window!" the face demanded.

Jorinda shook her head and crawled backward across the floor.

"Jorinda! Open the window!"

She was getting nearer and nearer the door.

BANG.

The face screamed, "I won't leave you!"

Jorinda stopped crawling. The face was Joringel's. Jorinda

leaped to her feet and ran to the window. "What are you doing out there?" she cried.

"They're taking the castle!"

Jorinda struggled with the window latch.

BANG.

Her shaking fingers fumbled with the heavy lead. Finally, she unstuck it and threw the window open. "Come in!" she cried. "Hurry!"

But Joringel shook his head. "No," he said. "You come out."

"What?"

"They're inside the castle already. There's fighting in the corridors. We can't get out that way."

"Then how can we get out?"

Joringel pointed down the castle walls. "Hold on to the stones, climb from window to window, and we can get to the Kingswood out back."

Jorinda looked down. It was a straight drop. "You're crazy!"

"Come on!"

"Aren't you scared?"

Joringel almost smiled. He nodded. But he held his hand out to his sister.

So she took it and pulled herself up onto the windowsill.

BANG.

The whole castle shook. Jorinda screamed and grabbed hold of the swinging shutters. "What's happening?" she panted, refusing to look down.

"They're breaking down the gates to let the rest of the army inside."

BANG—CRRRACK.

"They're through?" Jorinda asked, still holding on to the window for dear life.

A mighty roar erupted below them. The horses and soldiers and torch-wielding peasants surged forward.

"They're through," Joringel replied. "Come on! Let's go!"

And so Jorinda and Joringel, brother and sister, queen and self-appointed protector of the children of Grimm, climbed down the walls of the castle, dropped to the ground behind a green hedge, and ran with every ounce of strength they had deep, deep into the forest.

The Märchenwald

Once upon a time, two children collapsed to the ground under a great oak tree.

Jorinda and Joringel gasped at the dark air like drowning men, their lungs aching. Torches wove through the wood like great, frantic fireflies. They were still a distance off. But they were getting closer.

"We've got to keep moving," Jorinda heaved.

Joringel shook his head *no* and gulped the night into his lungs.

Jorinda, watching the torches, said, "Do you think it was the prince?"

Joringel, still sucking air, nodded.

The cries of the men were getting louder. And louder.

Jorinda pulled herself to her feet. "It's time—"

The words died away on her lips. Standing in the darkness at the edge of the clearing was a shadow. Even in silhouette, Jorinda could see that it was tall and lean and muscular.

And that it had a horn.

The creature stepped forward, and the moonlight shimmered on it. Despite herself, despite everything, Jorinda smiled. It was much larger than it had been. Its shoulders were broader, its haunches thicker. And the horn rising from its forehead was over a foot long.

"Is that . . . ?" Joringel stammered.

"Yes." His sister grinned. "That's a unicorn."

As if in response, the unicorn trotted forward and pressed its soft muzzle into Jorinda's neck. She felt a pang of bitter joy. It had been a year since she had seen her friend. A dark and bloody year.

In the deep forest, the torches were spreading out, fanning through the trees, moving in their direction. They could hear a voice barking orders.

The unicorn was nudging Jorinda's hand as if he wanted something. "I don't have any food for you," she whispered. The unicorn ducked his head, so that her arm was over his neck. She tried to push him away, saying, "We have to go! We have to—"

186

Suddenly, the unicorn knelt and pushed his body against Jorinda's, so that she was thrown over his back. She grabbed his mane.

Joringel laughed nervously. "I think he wants to give you a ride!"

"I think he does. Come on!" And she took her brother's hand and yanked him up behind her on the warm, wide back.

Without any warning, the unicorn sprang into the darkness, away from the approaching torches. His hooves pounded through the gloom, and Jorinda held tightly on to his mane, and Joringel wrapped his arms around her, and their legs squeezed the little unicorn's pulsing black flanks.

The wind whipped Jorinda's hair into Joringel's face, the branches slapped the children and snapped behind them, and the forest flew by in a blur.

The ride was half dream, half nightmare. Soon there were no torches. They passed out of the Kingswood. Far, far from any wood that either child had ever visited. But still, the unicorn rode on, now racing nothing but the moon.

At dawn, as the mist huddled in the trees like gray-clad monks, the unicorn slowed. The children gratefully, wearily, slid off his back.

Nearby, a brook burbled out of the fog, tumbled over stones, and disappeared into the fog again. The children fell to their stomachs and drank from its frigid, clear current.

Joringel sat back on his haunches. His mouth hurt from the cold, but the water tasted pure and good, liked melted snow. "Where are we?" he asked.

Jorinda wiped her sleeve across her face. "I don't know."

The unicorn shook himself and came and nuzzled up to Jorinda. She held his head. And then something sharp poked at the back of her mind.

She grimaced.

And she pushed the unicorn away.

He looked confused, staring at her with his wide, white eyes.

"Go!" Jorinda suddenly shouted. "Go home!"

The unicorn pawed the earth, as if to play their old game again.

"No!" Jorinda bellowed. "Leave! It's not safe!"

"Um, Jorinda? What are you doing?"

Jorinda was standing now, and shouting. "You have a family! You have a home! Go to them! Go now! GO!"

The little unicorn danced back and forth, pawing the earth in agitation. Still, Jorinda shouted at him, pushing his head away from her. At last, the little beast turned mournfully and disappeared into the mist.

"What did you do that for?" Joringel demanded. "Now we're lost!"

Jorinda did not look at him. She gazed into the fog that had swallowed the unicorn. "We've been lost," Jorinda said. "We've been lost for a long, long time."

She lay down by the riverbank. "I need to sleep."

Joringel stared at his sister. She pulled a fallen branch, thick with leaves, over her, but the fog didn't care. It crawled in through the thousand green gaps and wrapped Jorinda in a cold, wet quilt of gray. Joringel, too confused and exhausted to fight, leaned his back against a nearby tree and slid wearily to the ground.

In a moment, both children were asleep.

The morning was barely a morning. The mist was paler, as if somewhere, far, far above, a dim fire burned. The children stood, stretched, and shivered. Jorinda rubbed her thin arms up and down.

"Where are we?" Joringel asked, yawning through chattering teeth.

"I dunno," his sister replied. "But I'm hungry."

"I can't believe you told that unicorn to go away."

Jorinda shrugged. Hard. "It's not safe to be around me," she said. "Something bad happens to everyone and everything that comes near me."

Joringel looked at his hands and did not answer.

They decided to follow the stream. As they pushed farther and farther ahead, the mist began to lift. The forest looked familiar. Joringel, who had been walking ahead of his sister, came to a sharp stop.

"No," he murmured.

Jorinda walked up behind him. "What?"

Joringel was shaking his head. "No, no, no . . ."

"What is it?" she demanded.

He pointed. "The hunting lodge."

Jorinda looked. After a stunned moment, she said, "We didn't . . . ?"

"We didn't go anywhere," Joringel completed her thought. "We're still in the Kingswood."

Jorinda was squinting hard at the lodge. She started walking forward. Joringel tried to grab her, but she pulled her arm away.

"What are you doing?" he hissed. "Jorinda! They'll see you!"

"It looks like they repainted it," she said. "It used to be brown. Now it's green."

"Why do we care?" Joringel whispered. "They could paint it pink and yellow and call it Candy Land Hou—"

"LOOK!" Jorinda exclaimed. She was staring in the direction of the castle.

Joringel looked. One whole wing of the castle was missing.

"They destroyed it . . . ?" Joringel said. But there was no sign of fire, nor any rubble. Standing in its place was a garden. A full garden, in bloom. It looked as if that wing of the castle had never been built.

"What—?" Joringel stammered, "I . . . I don't understand . . ."

Jorinda started for the door to the kitchens.

All was quiet. Someone was cleaning up from the breakfast service. Nothing looked particularly out of order. Which was strange. Because last night there had been an invasion.

A kitchen maid bustled by, laden with dirty plates. "Excuse me!" she barked. Jorinda and Joringel stared as she went by.

"She didn't bow," Jorinda murmured.

"Or have us killed," Joringel added.

Cautiously, incredulously, they made their way from the kitchens up the back stairs, into the royal corridor. The décor was completely different than it had been, and everything looked newer, fresher.

They passed the chapel. Inside, a woman bent her head before the altar. Jorinda put an arm out and brought them both to a stop.

"She's wearing a crown," Jorinda whispered.

"Who is she?" her brother replied.

Even from the back, Jorinda was sure she didn't know. The children proceeded even more cautiously than before.

They passed many more doorways. The rooms looked strange. Finally, they came to the grand bedroom, where Jorinda had slept ever since she'd become queen. Both children stopped and peered from behind the doorjamb.

In the room, two children, smaller than Jorinda and Joringel, played at the foot of a bed. And a man with a beard and a crown on his head knelt beside the life-sized statue of a hideously ugly man.

The statue was speaking. Jorinda and Joringel stared, dumbstruck.

"There is a way, king, to rescue me from this rock, if you truly wish it," the statue said.

Jorinda and Joringel gaped at the talking statue.

"Oh, I do!" the bearded king cried. "I'll do anything! Anything!"

And the statue said . . .

There are no children in the room, right? You're certain? Okay . . .

————

ADAM GIDWITZ

Jorinda and Joringel stood straight up. They had heard a voice. A loud voice. It seemed to come from . . . everywhere. It had asked if there were children in the room. They looked at each other as if, perhaps, they were losing their minds.

The stone statue was speaking again. They looked back into the royal chamber.

"You must cut off the heads of your children, and smear my statue with their blood. And then, and only then, will I return to life."

Remember what I told you would happen when Hansel and Gretel finally showed up?

Jorinda and Joringel looked frantically all around them. Who had said that?

From the room, they heard the king say, "You under-stood me always, no matter what. So I will under-stand you."

The king drew a sword from its place on the wall, walked over to the two adorable children playing at the end of the bed, and swung the sword at their necks.

Jorinda and Joringel fell back into the hall as blood spattered across the floor. They froze. One second passed. Two. Three.

They ran. They flew down the hallway, past the bedrooms, down the stairs, through the kitchens, out the door, and into the Kingswood. They ran and ran and ran, and their little lungs could not get enough air, and they felt as if they were drowning.

They ran without thinking, without seeing, plunging past trees and logs and brambles, until the mist became heavier—so heavy that they could not see at all.

They fell to the ground and held each other, huddling in the cold fog. They could not say a word.

Jorinda and Joringel shivered in the mist for an hour or more. Then, in the distance, they heard the rumble of thunder. They peered into the gray soup overhead, waiting for the rain to follow. Thunder rumbled again, this time closer. The children huddled closer together. A third clap of thunder shook the leaves on the mist-shrouded trees.

"I felt that in my feet." Joringel swallowed.

Jorinda nodded. "It must be a big storm."

Another roll of thunder, and another, and another, closer and closer. The great trees shook.

And then, from the mist, emerged a mountain. That was the only way to describe it. A moving mountain of flesh. Pink

194   ADAM GIDWITZ

flesh. The mountain had a ridge like a backbone, and little valleys formed by small arms and legs, and a slope of a wide, flat tail. They could see thin black bones through the pink skin, and in the distended bag of a belly, black organs wound around one another, beating. And at either side of its huge, flat head sat two tiny black eyes.

The children could not move.

Each step the beast took made the whole forest tremble. Trees fell before it like weeds.

Suddenly, it stopped. Its little black eyes swiveled toward Jorinda and Joringel. The children stopped breathing. It cocked his head at the children. The children's hearts stopped beating. It opened his mouth. The children grabbed hold of one another.

Out of the beast's maw roared a column of flame. Jorinda and Joringel fell to the forest floor, eyes closed, holding each other tightly.

We are going to die, Joringel thought.

His sister, on the other hand, was pretty sure they were already dead.

A wall of fire pressed the children into the earth. They could not breathe, for the flame ate up all the oxygen. The mist above their heads had been replaced with reds and oranges and even one streak of pale aquamarine. Breathing, heartbeat, all vital functions had been shut down.

Dead, the children thought. *Dead, dead, dead.*

Gradually, the flame subsided. The two children did not move for a full minute. Then they looked up. The creature was staring at them from its tiny black eyes. It looked . . . curious.

"GO!" Jorinda screamed. The children leaped up and ran furiously, frantically, away from the beast. As their feet pounded the forest floor, they tried to listen for the thunderous footfall of the monster behind them. They heard nothing. This was good. They ran faster. Still, they did not breathe, nor were their hearts beating. Good: they did not need them.

They ran and ran and ran until they could run no more. Then the two little children collapsed to the ground and wept.

Okay, if you've read *A Tale Dark & Grimm* or *In a Glass Grimmly*, you are probably slightly confused right now.

If, on the other hand, you have not read either *A Tale Dark & Grimm* or *In a Glass Grimmly*, you are probably incredibly confused.

But don't worry! Neither Jorinda nor Joringel has read *A Tale Dark & Grimm* or *In a Glass Grimmly*, and they are *experiencing* what you are only reading about. So as confused as you might be, you've got nothing on them.

Jorinda and Joringel were under the cover of a wide, bushy hemlock. "Did you hear that?" Jorinda hissed.

Joringel was sitting straight as a ramrod. "I think someone is following us."

"It doesn't sound like someone is following us," Jorinda replied. "It sounds like someone is inside our heads."

"It's almost like the voice of God."

"But God keeps making stupid jokes."

"It knows our names."

"What's *In a Grass Glimmly?*" Jorinda asked.

"Or *Tall, Dark, and Grimm?*"

Jorinda shrugged. Then she peered out from behind the branches of hemlock. "Come on," she said. "I think it's clear." So the two children rose to their feet and pushed through the mist. It left trails of water on their cheeks and hung like raindrops from their eyelashes. They walked and walked and walked. And walked. And walked. Without being able to see more than three feet in front of them.

Images of decapitated children and fire-breathing monsters

danced before them in the mist. Also of closed doors. Of chests of apples. Of sisters riding away on horseback. Of groaning, miserable kingdoms.

Jorinda and Joringel tried to shove the thoughts down, cover them with mattresses, stamp them out, choke them back.

Neither child was succeeding.

At last, the mist began to thin, and the children slowed. They found themselves at the edge of a neatly maintained field. It had sharp, clean edges and white lines running along the grass.

At one end of the neat field was a very strange building. It was tall and kind of fat. Like a tower. But it was made of bright red brick. And there were other buildings like it. Many others. All around it. Near the building, at the other end of the field, children were sitting on the neatly mowed grass. Before them stood a young man. He appeared to be telling a story.

Jorinda started for him. Joringel followed. As they approached, his words became clearer.

They froze.

They knew that voice.

It was the voice they had been hearing in their heads.

It was saying,

Once upon a time, fairy tales were awesome . . .

Carriages without any horses zoomed by on the road.

ADAM GIDWITZ

Buildings made of brick and steel towered over the treetops. Jorinda's and Joringel's knees went weak. And the voice still echoed in their heads—perfectly in time with the tall, awkward guy talking to the seated children.

It was at this point that Jorinda and Joringel passed out.

The Märchenwald,
Part Two

O kay. You are confused. Very confused. I get that.

But please, trust me. Just give me a few minutes, and everything will be cleared up.

Jorinda and Joringel stared up at me, dumbstruck. Behind me, children—not wearing the garb of some long-ago kingdom, but instead dressed in blue jeans and T-shirts—ran around a classroom, laughing and pushing and shouting at one another. I ignored them.

"Where—?" Joringel blinked. He had no words.

"What—?" Jorinda's mouth stopped even trying.

You fainted. I brought you inside. I know this is very weird. But right now, I have to deal with my students, and then we can talk this all through. Okay?

The children nodded as if they didn't know what I was talking about.

Will you promise not to pass out again? At least until dismissal?

The children nodded again. I could have been asking them if they wanted to eat a wheelbarrow full of cat food. They were just going to keep nodding. I looked over my shoulder.

SAMMY!

A small boy named Sammy was kneeling in the block corner. My classroom had an excellent block corner, full of beautiful wooden blocks of all shapes and sizes. Sammy, a second grader with long blond hair and shining blue eyes, had just lifted up one of the longest, heaviest blocks in the room, pulled it behind his head, and was aiming it directly at another child's face.

***Sammy!* Do NOT do that!**

At which point, Sammy brought the block around with all the force he could muster. The child he was aiming at, luckily, ducked. Sammy, displeased, lifted the block again.

NO!

I was just about to sprint over to save the poor child from Sammy and his enormous block when I saw another student of mine. His name was George. George was dancing. On a table.

George! George, get down!

But George was not about to get down. He had just begun

his Michael Jackson impression, and he was moonwalking, very convincingly, across the tabletop.

That's not safe . . . I muttered. Yeah. He didn't care.

I looked to see how Sammy's target was faring, when I noticed Jeff. Jeff was a round boy with round glasses. He was in the arts and crafts area. I found that puzzling. Jeff was usually getting into trouble. What kind of trouble could you get into in the arts and crafts area? His back was to me. Suddenly, he turned around. Jeff had been gluing cotton balls *to his face.*

"I'm Santa Claus!" he shouted.

A few children cheered. I put my head in my hands. Jeff began to sing "Jingle Bells."

I walked to the rug at the center of the room. I sat down. I figured I would just watch the ensuing carnage. Sammy was chasing the poor kid around, waving the block over his head and screaming bloody murder. George had moved on to the groin grab in his Michael Jackson routine. Jeff was singing "Jingle bells, Batman smells, Robin laid an egg . . ."

Suddenly, I noticed that a few children had come to sit beside me on the rug. Bless these children. In every classroom, there are always three or four nice kids, who will help the teacher out, no matter how hopeless and unprepared that teacher might be. These four kids tucked their little legs into criss-cross-applesauce and gazed up at me, waiting for some kind of instruction.

I decided that I would let Sammy murder his classmate. I would let George moonwalk backward off a table. I would let Jeff develop a skin condition from the not-at-all skin-safe purple paste he was using on his face. Forget everyone else. I decided that I would just tell these four nice kids a story. And so I did. I said,

Once upon a time . . .

And then, the most amazing thing happened. Sammy suddenly stopped swinging his block. He looked at me.

Up on the table, George froze. And looked.

And over in the arts and crafts, Jeff—

Well, Jeff kept gluing cotton balls to his face.

I went on.

. . . **an old king lay on his deathbed. He was Hansel and Gretel's grandfather. But he didn't know that. Because Hansel and Gretel hadn't been born yet . . .**

As I told the story, I stopped to make jokes and to warn the second graders when something frightening was about to happen. Which was pretty often. Slowly, Sammy dropped his block, and started moving closer and closer to the rug. George sat down on the edge of the table and then moved down to the floor. And Jeff—kept gluing things to his face.

I told the children about a man called Faithful Johannes,

and about a young king and a golden princess, and their two little children, Hansel and Gretel. And then I told them about how, to save Johannes's life, the young king cut off Hansel's and Gretel's heads.

My students' mouths hung open. As did Jorinda's and Joringel's.

Then the school bell rang, and the kids all ran and got their coats and book bags and headed to the door. "Bye, Adam!" they cried. "See you tomorrow!" Sammy gave me a high five. I had no idea what I'd done to deserve a high five, except, perhaps, fail to intervene in his attempt at murder.

Once all the kids were gone, I took a deep breath, closed the classroom door, and turned to Jorinda and Joringel.

Well, I said. **You probably have some questions.**

"Yes," Jorinda nodded. "Do you have anything to eat?"

So I guided them to the rug, handed them two threadbare pillows, and offered them apple juice and animal crackers. Because that is the only food in the world a teacher is ever granted access to. But the children ate them hungrily.

At last, with crumbs speckling his mouth and half a cup of apple juice spilled down the front of his shirt, Joringel said, "Your voice . . . we've been hearing it in our heads."

Yeah, I'm sorry about that.

Jorinda shook herself like she had water in her ear. I apologized again.

"I have a question," said Joringel.

"I have a lot of questions," Jorinda added.

Okay. Go ahead.

"Well, what's that?" Joringel pointed at an old computer monitor that sat in the corner of the room.

Right. That would take me a really long time to explain.

"Oh."

Next question.

Jorinda asked, "Where are we?"

Well, right now it *looks* like we're in a classroom in Brooklyn, New York.

Jorinda blinked at me. "I have no idea what that means."

That's okay. Because, while it looks like we're in Brooklyn, we are actually in the Märchenwald.

Jorinda and Joringel both stared at me blankly.

You don't know what that means either, do you?

They shook their heads.

Well, *Märchen* means "story," or "fairy tale." And *Wald* means "forest." This is the Forest of Story.

Both children stared at me like I was a talking banana.

I tried again.

The Märchenwald is where all the stories in the world

ADAM GIDWITZ

are. Every story is told, and actually happens, here. When you fainted in that field, I was in the middle of telling a story from your world. And that story was happening elsewhere in this forest. Somewhere far away, other tales are being told and lived. All here. In the Märchenwald.

"What you're saying," Jorinda informed me, "doesn't make any sense."

Joringel said, "We saw a story you just told. The one about the two kids getting their heads cut off."

Yes. Hansel and Gretel.

"Right, well, we saw it happen."

Wow. That was probably upsetting.

"It was."

Well, don't worry. They come back to life.

"WHAT?"

"Um, how?"

I reached up to the shelf that sat beside my teacher's chair and pulled a slim blue book down from it. I held the book in my lap, looking at the cover. Jorinda and Joringel got to their knees and peered over my shoulder.

"A *Tale Dark and Grimm*," Joringel read aloud. "You said that when you were talking in our heads."

"What is it?" Jorinda asked.

This book has the whole story of Hansel and Gretel.

"Can we hear it?" Joringel asked. "Please?"

Well, maybe a little bit . . . I said. **Just so you know that Hansel and Gretel will be okay. Where should I start?**

"When they get their heads cut off!" Joringel shouted.

Jorinda looked sick. "How about just after that?"

So I cracked the spine of the book and began to read. After I finished the first chapter, the children wanted to hear the chapter after that. And, since I am unable to resist children who ask me for a story—I acquiesced. But when I finished the second chapter, the children wanted to hear the third. I said no, it had been a long day, and I was tired. But then they made those cute sad faces that kids make when they're really disappointed. Not the intentional, puppy-dog faces, which are annoying and have no effect on me whatsoever. Those let-down, looking-in-their-laps-and-sighing faces. So I read the third chapter.

By the end of that, we were hungry. And I was kind of enjoying myself. So I ordered pizza. As we waited for it, we read the fourth chapter. When it arrived, Jorinda and Joringel marveled at what was, to them, the greatest culinary invention in history.

After eating, we had plenty of energy, so we plowed through the fifth and sixth chapters. There are only nine chapters in the book, so once we were that close to the end, we decided just to finish it.

After I closed the book, Jorinda and Joringel sat in silence.

"Where was the pink monster?" Jorinda suddenly demanded. "Is that from one of your stories, too?"

Yes. That's from a different book I wrote. Called *In a Glass Grimmly*.

The children's eyes went wide. "Can we hear that?" Jorinda asked.

I'm not sure . . .

"Is it as bloody as the first one?" Joringel wanted to know.

Maybe worse . . .

"Perfect!" Joringel cried. "We've got enough pizza left to last us till morning!"

I have to teach tomorrow morning! I need some sleep.

The children looked down in their laps and sighed.

Fine.

I pulled a thicker yellow book down from the shelf above my teacher chair.

Ready?

The children pulled themselves up next to me and nodded. And I began.

We read chapter after chapter after chapter, as the Brooklyn streets outside the classroom window became darker and quieter and the sounds of traffic died away. Soon, all that could be heard from the deserted roads was the occasional wail of a siren, or the hissing groan of a garbage truck. My eyelids drooped—but every time I paused in my reading, the children poked me with their small, sharp fingers. I batted their hands away, scowled at them, and read on. At last, we came to that great pink monster, the Eidechse von Feuer, der Menschenfleischefressende. Also known as Eddie. I read:

"**They were staring at a small mountain that sat beside the winding lava river. The mountain was made not of rock, nor of magma, but of pink, fleshy skin. The mountain had a ridge like a backbone, and little valleys formed by small arms and legs, and a slope of a wide, flat tail. There was no head. But its body rose and fell with breath. They could see thin black bones through the pink skin, and in the distended bag of a belly, black organs wound around one another, pulsing.**"

"That's it! That's what we saw!" Joringel cried.

"It's gonna *kill* them," murmured Jorinda.

"They . . . they won't die, right, Adam?" Joringel asked me.

Instead of answering, I kept reading. I read to them about the frog translating Eddie's roars, and Eddie asking questions like, "Am I smelly? Very smelly? Is smelly good, or is smelly bad?" And then I told about how he helped the children escape the goblins by emerging from his giant hole and raining fire down upon the goblin soldiers and cities. Jorinda and Joringel cheered.

"He was nice!" Jorinda exclaimed at the end of the chapter.

"I like Eddie," Joringel agreed.

I smiled. **Everyone likes Eddie. He's the best.**

"Is he really?"

Yes. He really is.

"I want to meet him again. I won't be so scared this time."

Well, if you want to meet him, you have to learn how to say his name.

"Teach us!"

Sure. Ready?

They nodded.

Repeat after me: I-DECK-SUH VON FOY-ER DARE MEN-CHEN-FLYSH-FRESS-EN-DUH.

The children repeated after me.

Good. Now you'll be sure to meet him.

"Really?" Jorinda and Joringel asked at once.

I smiled. **Maybe.**

The children stared off into the distance. I continued reading. We read until the Brooklyn streets grew gray with dawn, and the birdsong was louder than the sirens, and you could smell the guy starting to roast his coffee in his stand on the corner. At last, we finished the book.

The children smiled up at me. "I liked the first one better," Joringel announced.

I chuckled.

"I have a question," Jorinda murmured. "Why would you tell your students such a horrible story?"

Hm. That's a good question. I thought about it for a minute. **I think it's because I like to scare children.**

"That's awful!" Jorinda exclaimed.

No, scaring children is fun. But there's another reason I'm telling these stories. In addition to enjoying scaring the bejeezus out of children.

The children looked up at me expectantly.

I took a deep breath. **I tell these stories because everything that happens in them not only happened to Hansel and Gretel and Jack and Jill. It also all happened to me.**

Joringel sat up like a bolt. "You got your head cut off by your parents, too?"

You want to see the scar?

Both children's eyes went wide. I lowered the collar of my shirt. They leaned forward . . .

I'm just kidding. There's no scar.

They both exhaled.

No, my parents didn't cut off my head . . . At least, not physically.

ADAM GIDWITZ

The children squinted. "Then how?"

Well, think about it this way. How would you feel if your parents cut off your heads to save some old friend of theirs? And then your head got put back on—but they didn't know that was going to happen? How would you feel about them, and your relationship with them?

"I'd feel angry," said Jorinda.

"I'd want to cut their heads off back!" Joringel announced.

"And betrayed," Jorinda continued.

"I'd put them in a pot of boiling oil . . ." said Joringel.

"I'd feel like they didn't love me enough," decided Jorinda.

". . . with snakes in it! Yeah, snakes!" Joringel cried.

"I'd feel like maybe they cared about their friend more than me," Jorinda concluded.

"Then, I'd put them in a barrel, and I'd drive nails into it, and I'd roll it down a hill!" bellowed Joringel.

Okay, Joringel, I get it. You'd want revenge.

"Revenge!" he shouted, raising his small fists in the air.

So you'd feel angry, betrayed, like they didn't love you, like they cared for someone else more than they cared for you, like you wanted revenge . . .

The children nodded.

I hope you've never felt that way about your own parents.

Jorinda and Joringel suddenly looked intensely uncomfortable. Joringel discovered something interesting just over my shoulder. Jorinda stared into her lap.

But I know that I have.

They looked at me again.

You see, my parents never cut off my head *physically*. I paused. **But maybe *emotionally*.**

Do you know what I mean?

I could see in the children's faces that they were wrestling with something, deep inside themselves. Something that churned heavily, bubbling and roiling like a great, filthy sea. After a moment, Jorinda asked, "What did they do to you?"

I sighed. **What do parents ever do to kids? Most parents love their children and try to take care of them the best that they can. But parents mess up, all the time.**

Joringel was staring away from me as hard as he could. But Jorinda insisted, "What did they do though?"

I bit my lip. **Well, I suppose the thing that they did that made me feel most betrayed and angry and not cared for was when they got divorced. It hurt. A lot. So I tell stories about it. Crazy stories with blood and death and talking birds. To help me understand it. To help me feel it.**

The room was perfectly silent.

At last, Joringel said, "Why would you want to feel it?"

"Yeah," Jorinda agreed. "You just need to smother it."

"Stamp it out."

"Choke it back."

I smiled sadly. **Does that seem true to you?** My gaze traveled between the two children. **Does that help you stop feeling the pain?**

There was another moment of silence. Of a quivering quiet in the room.

Memories pressed down upon the two children. Closed doors. Chests of apples. Birds and stepsisters and princes on horseback. Their faces flushed. Jorinda's nostrils trembled. Joringel was holding his reddening eyes open unnaturally wide.

Does it?

And then, the wave came crashing down upon Jorinda and Joringel. I could see it. I could see them bracing themselves against the cold, muddy waters inside them. I could see them buckle. I could see them trying not to drown.

Emotions rise. They churn in your stomach. They grip your windpipe. They make you do things you never thought you would.

The children fought it all valiantly.

Just remember:

There are all sorts of things you can do with a stone besides smothering it.

When you stamp on weeds, they just grow back—and you're killing everything else in the field.

And oceans are not only for drowning in.

Jorinda and Joringel sat in silence.

After a moment, Jorinda said, "I have no idea what any of that means."

I grinned. **All I'm trying to say is that it's okay to feel things sometimes. In fact, I think feeling things—even painful things—can be good.**

The morning was now bright and busy outside the classroom window. Women in suits and men in uniforms hurried by on the street, eating egg sandwiches or shouting into their phones.

Well, the students are going to show up soon. I had neither prepared for the school day nor even showered. Which, it must be admitted, was kind of typical for me. Still, I was going to feel better if I could wash up in the bathroom before Sammy recommenced his murderous spree and George began dancing on the tables and Jeff started working on his incipient skin condition. I stood up and stretched. **I think I ought to take you back home now.**

The children nodded sleepily.

I walked them out of the school, back across the field, and to the small stand of trees. They gazed at the cars zooming by and

ADAM GIDWITZ

the tall buildings of downtown Brooklyn. Pigeons and sparrows fought in the dirt nearby over a hot-dog bun. Neither child spoke.

Well . . . I said at last. **It's been nice meeting you.**

Joringel reached out to shake my hand. I took it, but then pulled him in for a hug.

I turned to Jorinda. She looked like she was trying to work something out. And indeed, she said, "If we're all in the Märchenwald right now, does that mean we're all in a story?"

I hesitated. **I . . . I don't *think* so.**

I hugged Jorinda, too. But when she turned away from me, I could tell that she was still thinking about it.

Then the two children took each other's hand and returned to the misty wood.

Jorinda and Joringel trudged through the cold fog that speckled their faces with water, wading through creeks and clambering over brambles.

"Is this really . . ." Joringel began, trailing behind his sister through the wood, "whatever he called it? The Marching Vault? The Story Forest?"

Jorinda shook her head. "How could it be?" She clambered over a rotten log. "Everyone we meet is just a character in a story? It makes no sense."

"Yeah," Joringel agreed. "Crazy. I think that guy had a problem."

The children walked on without speaking for a long time. At last, Joringel asked, "What do you think of the other stuff he said, though?"

"What?"

"You know. About stones and weeds and oceans and stuff."

"Oh. I don't know." Suddenly, tears poked at the sides of her eyes. She wiped them away quickly. "I don't know."

They trudged on. The mist began to dissipate. The sun was still obscured by gray, but at least they could tell where it was now. They felt, very faintly, its warmth.

Joringel turned to his sister. He took a deep breath. He held it. And then he said, "Jorinda, if you won't leave me, I won't leave you."

Jorinda pursed her lips into a small red rose. Something bubbled and roiled inside her. "I will never, ever leave you," she said.

Joringel smiled.

And Jorinda added. "Ever."

Which was a very nice thing to say.

Sadly, though, it was not true.

For just at that moment, they heard the sound of hooves, pounding through the wood.

The children turned.

From the wood emerged three unicorns, each black as midnight and foaming sweat. In the lead was the little one, followed by two larger beasts, both with long, twining horns and wide eyes.

There was something wrong.

The unicorns pounded past them. "Hey!" Jorinda cried. She tried to follow.

But Joringel grabbed her sleeve. "Little Sister . . ." he whispered.

She turned back to him. Her eyes went wide.

Pounding through the wood after the unicorns came a dozen white horses, each carrying a rider with a lance and a bow slung across his back. The riders prodded their mounts with bloody spurs and exhorted one another to hurry. At the center of the group rode Herzlos.

"STOP!" Jorinda screamed.

Joringel yanked his sister to the ground behind a thick

hemlock bush. "Shhh!" he hissed. "They'll kill us!"

"STOP!" Jorinda cried. She shoved her brother away. "They'll kill the unicorns! STOP!" She leaped to her feet and went running after the tyrant Herzlos. "STOP!"

As the horses cantered forward, Herzlos glanced over his shoulder at the little girl screaming and running after him.

He pulled up. He turned his horse around. He was staring at Jorinda. The other horsemen reined their steeds around to see what Herzlos was after, as the unicorns galloped away. Herzlos's black hair hung down over his smug, scarred face.

Jorinda glared.

Suddenly, Herzlos's bloody spurs jabbed at his steed's side, and the beast catapulted forward.

Joringel, still lying behind the hemlock, screamed.

The tyrant's horse barreled ahead, and he lowered his lance, and tucked his chin, and squinted.

Jorinda flinched.

And just then, Herzlos's lance went straight through Jorinda's chest and came out the other side.

Red blood spattered the green ferns of the forest floor.

The little girl was still standing.

For a moment.

Then she fell.

Jorinda lay on the brambled ground. She was no more than a crumpled body, a lance through her chest, blood seeping into her clothes, her eyes wide, her face still.

Herzlos reined his charger, threw back his black hair, and smiled.

Without a sound, Joringel turned and fled into the wood.

Then, as he ran, he began to scream.

I don't know what to say.

I'm sorry.

I . . . I'm sorry.

Hell

Once upon a time, a little boy crouched amid tall, dark bushes. Overhead, birds sang as if nothing at all had happened. As if the one-time queen of Grimm had not just been murdered. As if the center of a clearing nearby was not smeared with her blood. As if the greedy flies were not buzzing around her corpse, sizing up their next meal.

Joringel bent over and was sick on the ground for the fourth time in as many minutes. Then he wiped his mouth and held himself and rocked back and forth under a little shelter of branches.

"Wowza," said a reedy voice just above Joringel's head.

"Tough," said another.

"That's an understatement," said a third.

Joringel looked up. Three ravens were perched in the upper branches of the dark green bushes, peering down sympathetically at him.

Joringel wiped both cheeks and his nose on his sleeve. He sniffed, which made him cough, which then made him be sick all over the ground again.

"Maybe we should come back later," said the first raven.

Joringel wiped his face again and shook his head.

"Help me," he said.

"We're really not supposed to," said the first raven.

"It's against the rules," said the second.

The third said, "Besides, what kind of help do you want? She's dead."

Joringel's face was iron. "Help me get her back."

"Um, did you hear my brother?" the first raven said. "She's *dead*."

"Gone."

"Deceased."

"She is an *ex*-person."

"But where did she go?" Joringel demanded. "Which way?" He pointed up with one hand and down with the other.

The three ravens started coughing and looking anywhere

that wasn't the boy. "We don't know," said one awkwardly. "Hard to say," said another. "Not really our domain," said a third.

"She went down, didn't she? She went to Hell."

"Well, at least he guessed it," said the first, relieved.

"Yeah, I didn't want to have to tell him."

"Me neither."

You know why she went down, right?

Because that's what happens to tyrants.

Even little girl tyrants.

(Not that there are a whole lot of those.)

Joringel put his face in his hands. His eyes were hard and brittle like ice. After a moment, he said, "I want to go get her."

The three ravens stared at the little boy.

"Wouldn't be prudent," said the first.

"Wouldn't be possible," clarified the second.

"Hansel did it," said Joringel. "He went to Hell and came back. Remember?"

The three ravens did a double take.

"What?"

"You know about that?"

Joringel said, "I read it in A *Tale Dark and Grimm*."

The third raven blinked at the little boy. "The metafictional dimensions of that statement are kind of blowing my mind."

"I don't know what that means," Joringel replied. "But I do know that it's possible to go to Hell and come back alive."

"That's only the first challenge," the first raven reminded him. "Retrieving someone who's already dead is a challenge of a different order entirely."

"That means it's way harder," his brother put in.

"Well, I'm going to do it," Joringel proclaimed. "And I need your help."

"What can we do?" the first raven asked. "It's not like we can bring people back from the dead."

"It's not really our *field*," the second agreed.

"Thankfully," added the third. "I am definitely afraid of dead people."

"Just show me," Joringel begged them. "Just show me where it is."

"Hell?"

"You want to know where Hell is?"

"He wants *directions*?" The third raven looked at his brothers and then back at the little boy. He shrugged. "*That* we could do."

It was a harrowing journey. Joringel followed the flight of the ravens through forests thick with brambles. He nearly froze to death during the nights on snowy promontories of mountains. He was swept away by a great river and lay, choking, on a bank half a mile downstream.

Finally, he found himself in the midst of rolling green hills. The sky was bright and blue above, the sun beamed warm and gentle on his neck, and the breeze whispered in the tall grass. The ravens were facing away from him, perched on top of a hill.

"How much farther?" the boy asked as he approached.

The ravens turned their black beaks over their shoulders. "Not much," said the first. "Come here."

Joringel circumnavigated the hill. When he reached the opposite face, his eyes went wide. Before him stood doors that were as tall and black and smooth as eternity, nestled into the bright green hill as if they were the most natural thing in the world.

"So? What's the plan?" asked the first raven.

"Yeah," said the second, "it's not like you can just walk in."

"What do I have to do?" asked Joringel, his eyes fixed on the doors.

"Well, you have to knock," said the first raven.

"And then?"

"And then a demon will probably appear. And he'll probably ask you what you want."

"And then?"

"And then we've got no clue, kid!" the third raven exclaimed. "This was *your* bright idea!"

"You could always try to get in the normal way," suggested the second raven. "You know, jumping off a cliff, or stabbing yourself in the face with a sword, or kicking a pregnant bear—"

"That's normal?" said the third raven.

"But if you got into Hell that way, you'd never get out again," the first raven went on. "And it would be indescribable torture for all eternity."

"Pits of fire?" Joringel asked, remembering Hansel's journey.

"Maybe. Or maybe not. That's the beauty of Hell. The Devil's a clever lad. Whatever *you* think the worst possible torture would be—that's what you get. It's personally tailored to your worst nightmare."

The three ravens watched the little boy in silence. He was frowning and staring at the tall obsidian portal. He shoved his hands into his pockets. His brow furrowed. He dug around in his left pocket, fingering something. And then, he smiled.

Joringel reached out his hand and knocked on the smooth black doors of Hell.

The doors screamed as they opened. Not, like, their hinges squealed. Like, the doors were screaming. The sudden sound sent the ravens fluttering off of the hill, a burst of black wings that rose into the blue sky.

Standing just inside the door, shrouded by darkness, was a bony creature. It had a large, round head and leering, wet eyes. It wore no clothes over its ashen skin. In its right hand it held a fire iron, its tip glowing orange. The demon smiled. "Are we expecting you?" it asked. Its voice sounded like shards of broken glass scraping against a mirror.

Joringel shook his head. "I— I don't think so."

The demon's smile turned into an ugly scowl. "Then you can't come in!"

Joringel withdrew his hand from his left pocket. In his palm sat a little monkey, carved from ivory.

He held it out to the demon.

"What?" the ashen demon demanded.

"Do you see what I have?" Joringel asked.

The demon squinted at it. "Yeah, very nice. But you still can't come in."

"Do you *see* it?" Joringel insisted.

The demon looked again. "Yeah. It's a cute ivory monkey, but—"

Suddenly, his eyes went wide, he stood straight up, his body became stiff as a board, and then he toppled over backward.

Joringel took a deep breath.

Then he stepped into the darkness of Hell.

The doors screamed shut behind him. It was perfectly dark. Perfectly. As if black velvet curtains had been dropped over Joringel's head. The only illumination at all came from the floor where the glowing fire iron lay. Joringel bent over, scooped it up, and held it aloft. The gloom was so thick, so solid, that Joringel could see nothing.

He waved the glowing tip of the fire iron toward the ground until he located the demon, propped up on one elbow, rubbing his head.

The demon blinked woozily at the little boy through the deep gloom. "Who are you? What do you want?"

"I want my sister, Jorinda," Joringel announced.

"You can't have her," the demon replied.

Joringel's knuckles whitened around the fire iron. Wasn't the demon supposed to obey him now? He licked his dry lips. "I can't have her?" The impenetrable darkness seemed to swallow up his words.

"No," the demon groaned, pulling himself to his feet. "What happened to me, anyway?"

"You fell down," said Joringel. "Stand up."

The demon pulled himself to his feet.

"Jump up and down," Joringel commanded.

The demon began to jump up and down.

"Slap yourself in the face."

The demon continued to jump up and down and began slapping himself in the face.

"Now release my sister."

The skinny, ashen demon continued jumping up and down in the heavy dark and slapping himself in the face. "I can't."

"Why not?"

"Only the Devil can release sinners."

"Then take me to the Devil."

"Are you sure? He's not the nicest guy in the world. Or below it." The demon was still jumping up and down and slapping himself in the face.

"I can handle him," Joringel said.

The demon smirked. "Sure you can." And then he went hopping away from Joringel into the darkness. The little boy trailed with the glowing fire iron, following the sound of a demon slapping himself over and over and over again.

"Um . . . excuse me . . ." Joringel called ahead. "You . . . uh . . . you can stop that . . ."

Somewhere far above Joringel's head, water dripped onto stone. Joringel held the poker out before him with one arm, and with the other he hugged himself, for the air was frigid. Rancid, too. A pungent musk assaulted the little boy as he walked. He tried not to breathe it in too deeply. It reminded him of something. What was it? Oh, yes. Smoke, rising from a millstone.

Suddenly, the glow of the fire iron came upon something. Joringel was not sure what this something was, as it was just as black as the air around it. But it had shape. He traced its silhouette with the glowing iron. It seemed to be an enormous, black egg.

"Hey!" Joringel called to his demon guide. "What's this?"

He heard the demon's footsteps slow and turn. In a moment, the ghastly, emaciated face was beside his own.

"Sinner." The demon grinned.

Joringel squinted his eyes at the darkness. "Where?"

"Here!" Suddenly, the demon made a grab for the fire iron. The demon's sinewy hands wrestled the metal rod away from Joringel, sending the boy stumbling backward.

"Stop!" Joringel cried. "Don't hurt me! I command you!"

He could just see the demon's face in the light of the glowing iron. The demon was leering at him. "I wasn't," the demon smirked. "I was going to show you the sinner." And with that, he guided the fire iron over the rest of the black, shadowy egg.

There was someone inside. It was a man. He was old, with a long, gray beard and a bald pate. He seemed to be shouting, though Joringel could hear nothing. The old man shouted, and his hands pushed at the inside of the egg. They pushed and pushed, and then the old man balled them into fists and beat the ovoid walls around him. At last, he gave up. He bowed his head. Suddenly, he arched his back and howled in agony. Joringel didn't hear a sound.

"That's awful . . ." Joringel murmured.

The demon grinned. "Isn't it? Alone. For all eternity. No one cares. No one looks in on you. That's it. Alone."

Joringel's stomach lurched sickeningly.

"You don't think it's so bad?" the demon asked, misinterpreting Joringel's expression. "It's not—for the first few hours." The demon's smile grew. "But then panic sets in. You'd think they'd be lonely. Or sad. And they are. Horribly. Crushingly. But really, it's the panic that's the worst. It never leaves you. Something about humans and being alone . . ." The demon thought about this. Clearly, it made him happy.

The demon led Joringel on. As they walked, the demon used the fire iron to illuminate the dark eggs. After a while, they came to two, right next to one another. Inside, two young women writhed and wept. They had no eyes, and their faces were hideously scarred.

Joringel said, "Wait." His demon guide turned and waited. "What was their sin?"

The demon replied, "Those two? Let me think . . ." He tapped his chin. "Ah, yes! I remember! They are here for their vanity, their cruelty, their selfishness, and their falseness. Do you know they were willing to cut off pieces of their feet just to fool a prince into marrying them? Can you believe it?"

Joringel watched them writhe. They seemed to be calling out. But Joringel could not hear them. No one could. No one would, ever again.

He began to feel dizzy. The cold wrapped around him, yet sweat poured down his brow. The dark eggs stretched on, and on, and on.

They came to another one. Inside this egg, a bearded man wore a broken crown. He wept and beat at his cage and yanked the hair from his beard. Joringel thought he recognized him. Then he remembered. He had been the king of Grimm. Before Jorinda had taken over.

Joringel turned away, frantically trying to catch his breath. The darkness closed in on him. He could not breathe. The demon led him on. Joringel scoured the shadowy cocoons avidly, desperately. He peered into the darkness as if seeking some great secret, some respite from the eternal pain.

But that wasn't what he was looking for.

He was looking for Jorinda.

Plutonic Gardens

Once upon a time, a little boy followed a hunched, bony, bald-headed demon through the gloom of Hell.

They had emerged from among the shadowy eggs, and the darkness had lifted a little. Now, the road they followed was broad and flat. They came to a gate, with a small guardhouse and a white barrier across the road. Next to the barrier was a sign that read WELCOME TO PLUTONIC GARDENS.

The demon punched some buttons on a keypad, and the barrier lifted. Joringel followed the demon down the road and past a field. But it was unlike any field Joringel had ever seen. It had short grass and random pits of sand and tiny flags waving from thin poles. It was weird. They then passed the strangest lake Joringel had ever seen. The water was an unnatural blue, and its edges were neat and clean and squared off. A sign read NO RUNNING, NO EATING, NO HORSEPLAY, NO DIVING. Horses were not allowed to play in the lake? Joringel was very confused.

On either side of the road stood houses, each virtually identical. Before each house stood a sculpture of a strange looking bird, with one leg and a black beak and a body that was painted entirely pink. From time to time, they passed street signs, which read things like DEADLY NIGHTSHADE DRIVE and HEMLOCK COURT and POISON IVY PLACE.

"Where are we?" Joringel whispered.

"It's a new development," the demon grumbled, rolling his eyes. "Tacky, if you ask me." The demon turned onto a flat path and led Joringel up to the door of a small, low-slung black house.

Joringel turned to the demon. "This is where the Devil lives?"

"It's his grandmother's, actually. On his father's side. He used to live with the other one, but they had a falling out about seven generations ago. Something about someone wearing her clothing . . ."

"Oh." Joringel smiled. "Right."

"Anyway," continued the demon, standing under the eaves of the jet-black ranch-style home. "I think it's kind of nice he lives with his grandmother. You'd think he'd want something grander, given that he's the Prince of Darkness and all. But he's a simple soul. With simple tastes."

"Like what?"

"Oh, causing eternal, excruciating, unbearable suffering."

"And . . . ?"

"And that's about it. Well," said the demon, "he's all yours!" And he went hurrying down the path away from the house.

Joringel turned stiffly to the little black door. He wiped the sweat from his palms on his pants and gauged the situation.

On the door was a knocker. It looked like the bronzed head of a baby. Joringel looked closer. It *was* the bronzed head of a baby. Joringel turned around and tried not to throw up.

Joringel staggered down the front steps of the house. He decided to circle around to the nearest window, to get the lay of the land. Joringel tiptoed up and peered through the pane. He was looking at a living room. Sort of like a normal living room. There was a simple, modern-looking table. It was carved from bone. This disturbed Joringel. But not nearly so much as the red rug that the table sat on. The rug was tongues. Stitched together, human tongues.

Suddenly, a rather large elderly woman tottered into view. She had pale, reddish skin, thick black lipstick, and a huge cone of orange hair. It looked, in fact, like she had painted a beehive orange and placed it on top of her head. The old woman slowly, with great effort, bent her ample form to pick up a pillow that was lying on the rug and put it back on the couch. Both the pillow and the couch were made of scalps.

Joringel ducked away from the window and went back to the front door. He wiped the sweat from his forehead with his sleeve and did his best to dry his perspiring palms. Then he reached out, grabbed the bronzed head of the baby, and rapped it against the door.

"Hold on a minute!" It was the old woman's voice. He heard her mumbling as she made her way to the door. "A visitor? Who would visit? Maybe Lukey lost his keys? He's always forgetting something—"

The door swung open, revealing the old woman.

She gaped at Joringel. "Who are you?"

"Hi," said Joringel, smiling as innocently as he could. "I'm Joringel. I'm here to see the Devil."

The devil-woman squinted at him. "You want to see Lukey? I should have known. No one ever comes to see me anymore. There was a time! So many men, you wouldn't *believe*. There was a time when men would line up around the *block* to ask me to the movies, take me on Coke dates, take me into the backseats of their cars. They worshipped me!"

Joringel didn't know what movies or a Coke date or a car was. He shifted uneasily from foot to foot and looked down the lane to see if anyone was coming.

"Now? Nobody," the old woman went on. "I guess it's because I'm old. No one cares about an old woman. An ugly old woman. BEWARE!" she shouted suddenly.

Joringel jumped a foot.

"BEWARE! One day you, too, will be old and ugly! And your grandson won't come home for lunch ever! *Ever!* BEWARE!

Joringel dug in his pocket. "I brought you something," he said.

"For who? For me?"

"Yes."

"I don't believe you. Nobody brings me anything anymore. There was a time! So many men, you wouldn't *believe*—"

"Look," said Joringel. And he held the little monkey in his hand.

"Ooh!" the old woman exclaimed. "Ooh, it's adorable! What an adorably cute little monkey!"

And then her eyes rolled back in her head, and she went stiff as a board, and she fell over backward.

Joringel stepped inside and closed the door to the Devil's house.

When the Devil's grandmother came to, Joringel was crouching over her.

"When is your grandson coming home?"

"Who knows?" she moaned, rubbing her head. Then she said, "Why am I lying on the floor?"

"You fell down," said Joringel. He helped her up.

"Well?" the Devil's grandmother asked. "Are you staying for dinner?"

"Will the Devil be here?"

"We should be so lucky."

Joringel didn't know what that meant.

"And do you know I made brisket! Of babies! He loves baby brisket! So he probably won't come home until it's cold and dried out! He could at least *call*."

Joringel tried to make sense of what she was saying. "Okay, so he's supposed to come home for dinner?"

"Supposed to? *Supposed* to. Let me tell you—"

"I'm going to go hide," Joringel interrupted her. "When he does come home, you will tell him that I'm your guest, and that I'll be having dinner with you."

"I didn't make enough brisket!"

"That's okay," Joringel assured her. "I won't actually eat any."

"Your mother will be upset."

Joringel ignored her. "When you've told him about me, call me and I'll come out. Tell him he *must* be nice to me. No damning me to torment or anything like that. Understand? Now, where should I hide?"

The old woman showed Joringel a narrow staircase that led to an attic. Joringel climbed the dusty stairs and found himself in a crawl space between the downstairs ceiling and the roof. It was littered with some of the most outlandish, grotesque objects he had ever seen. There was a head with a crown still attached, a stuffed little boy with a lollipop all the way up his nose, and a pile of kidneys, still warm. He tried not to look. He also tried not to think of Jorinda. And he tried not to think about the fact that he was about to meet the Devil. In his own house. He listened for the front door.

Soon, he heard it open and heard the Devil cry, "Grandmother, I'm home!"

Joringel waited. He did not breathe. Muffled voices rose up the narrow stair. And then, after a minute, the grandmother cried, "All right! It's okay! Come on down!"

Joringel approached the dusty stairs. His heart was beating so hard he could hear it. He peered down to the foot of the staircase.

The Devil was waiting for him.

The Devil was a tall man, with reddish skin, a pointed beard, spectacles that sat on the end of his nose, and a thousand strands of shining, golden hair. He was peering at Joringel through his little glasses.

"See? I told you he was strange looking," his grandmother whispered so loudly that the neighbors could hear it. "Not the *most* handsome, if you want my opinion."

The Devil pursed his lips. "And this is . . . your guest?" He looked incredulous.

"Oh yes, dear, and you must be nice to him. He's having dinner with us. It's brisket. But he's not having any. His mother will be very upset."

"I'm sure she will be," the Devil said. He approached Joringel. He bent down until their faces were right next to each other. Joringel could feel the heat radiating off the Devil's skin. "How, exactly, do you know my grandmother?"

Joringel smiled. "Old friends." A line of sweat slid down his face.

"Old friends from where?" The Devil's voice was rich and dark and haughty.

"We used to go to the movies," Joringel replied.

ADAM GIDWITZ

The Devil did not know what to say to that.

"Time for dinner!" the grandmother announced. She led the way into the kitchen. The Devil gestured for Joringel to go first. His red eyes tracked the boy's every move.

Three places were set at the table. Joringel saw the cutlery was made of human bones and teeth. He did not touch it.

The grandmother cut a big slab of brisket for the Devil, and then took a tiny sliver for herself. "Are you sure you won't have some?" she asked Joringel. "We could spare a little."

"No!" Joringel exclaimed. "I mean—no thank you."

The Devil was already eating hungrily.

"I have a question," said Joringel.

The Devil raised his eyebrows.

"Does everyone get the same punishment here in Hell? Those eggs for everyone?"

The Devil sat back contentedly. He was always happy to discuss his favorite subject: Torture. "That's what you see, is it? Not pits of fire? How interesting. Well, everyone's different. Cocoons of Solitude, I call them. Lovely little invention, if I do say so myself. But no, the cocoons are just for your run-of-the-mill sinner. Those people I don't particularly care for, but I don't *hate* either. There are a few people I really, really *hate*. And they get a special treatment."

"Like what?"

"Well, take this one girl who died recently," said the Devil.

Joringel sat straight up in his chair.

"She comes from a family that I have hated for seven generations, ever since one of them snuck into Hell and made a fool out of me."

Joringel's mind raced. Could he mean Jorinda? Was she— were they—related to Hansel and Gretel?

"She, too, gets a Cocoon of Solitude. But hers is worse than the rest."

"How . . . worse?"

The Devil smiled. "She gets to see the people she has loved. She can speak to them, too. She calls to them. But they never come to her. Some do not hear her. Others do—and ignore her. She will never understand why. She will be utterly neglected, utterly lonely—in the presence of those she loves."

Joringel's stomach twisted so hard he nearly cried out in pain.

The Devil's grandmother yawned. "Well, I'm bored." She got up from the table and began to clear the plates.

Joringel watched her as she turned her back on them. Then, with a trembling hand, he dug into his pocket.

"I wanted to show you something," he said. He withdrew his hand from his pocket and opened it.

The Devil looked from the corner of his eye. "Ah," he said. "Nice monkey."

"Cute, isn't it?" said Joringel.

The grandmother looked over her shoulder from the sink. Blood poured from the faucet. "Oh, it's *so* cute!"

"Yes," said Joringel. He turned to the Devil. "Wouldn't you say that it's cute?"

"Oh, yes," said the Devil. "I would say that."

"Say what?" asked Joringel.

The Devil frowned. "I would say that it's cute."

"You would say that *what's* cute?" Joringel asked. His hand was shaking noticeably.

"I would say that that monkey is cute," said the Devil, squinting suspiciously at the little boy.

It's not going to work, Joringel thought. *What was I thinking? It's a stupid plan. It's not going to work.*

The grandmother hobbled over from the sink, as crimson blood poured fluently into the basin. "Yes," she agreed, "it really is a cute ivory monkey." And then she stood up and started blinking rapidly. "Hey!" she cried, pointing at Joringel. "Who are you?"

The Devil looked very surprised.

Joringel held up the monkey. "Remember me?" he asked. He could barely breathe. He felt light-headed. "I brought you this?" The monkey was shaking in his hand like there was an earthquake.

The Devil's grandmother glared at the little carving. Then she said, "Right . . . you're the boy with that cute ivory monkey . . ." Suddenly, her eyes rolled back in her head, her body went stiff as a board, and she fell over.

"What the Hell!" cried the Devil. "What just happened?"

Joringel looked frantically back and forth between the Devil and his grandmother. The plan was failing. Utterly failing. "I-I think," he stammered, "I think she said something that made her fall over."

"Yes! I think she did!" cried the Devil, crouching over his grandmother.

"What was it?" Joringel asked.

The Devil looked up at Joringel. "You want *me* to say it?"

"Say what?" asked Joringel. The Devil could hear his heart beating. Joringel was sure of it.

"You want me to say what my grandmother just said?"

"What did your grandmother say?"

The Devil squinted at the little boy. "You know."

"What?"

"You know!"

"She said 'you know'?"

ADAM GIDWITZ

"No!" cried the Devil. "You know what she said!"

"What did she say?"

"You just want me to say it!" cried the Devil.

"Why would I want you to say 'it'?"

"No! You just want me to say 'cute ivory monkey'!"

Joringel breathed an enormous sigh of relief.

The Devil's eyes rolled back in his head, his body went straight as a board, and—

He grabbed Joringel by the throat.

Joringel dropped the monkey.

With one hand, the Devil held on to Joringel. With the other, he scooped up the ivory monkey from the floor.

Joringel was choking. The skin of his throat was burning. He could not breathe.

"You thought you could overpower me with this? With *this*?" The Devil grinned, brandishing the monkey in one hand, while the other was wrapped firmly around Joringel's neck. "The monkey is cute, I'll grant you. But it's a parlor trick, good for old ladies and mortals. Do you know who I am? I am the Prince of Darkness. I am the most powerful force under Heaven. Do not play with me, boy."

The Devil took a deep breath. Joringel was choking. The

Devil's grip tightened. "But I am glad you're here. Do you know how long I have been waiting for one of you to come back down here and try to fool me? Seven generations! Seven generations since your great-great-great-great-great grandfather dressed up like my maternal grandmother and made a fool out of me! Oh, I have been waiting for you. I have been waiting, little boy."

Joringel could barely hear what the Devil was saying. His vision was fading. His skin was burning and blistering under the Devil's hand.

"And now I shall punish you. I have a special punishment for you, just as I had for your sister. Do you know what it is?"

The Devil waited, as if Joringel would try to guess. Joringel could not breathe. Guessing was out of the question.

"No?" smiled the Devil. "Your punishment, boy, is to *watch her suffer*. You will get to watch your dear sister suffer *for all eternity*. And no matter what you do, no matter how good you are, no matter how many times you say 'please, pretty please with a cherry on top,' I will never, ever, *ever* let you out. It will be excruciating pain from now until eternity."

Joringel kicked his legs frantically. His lungs were collapsing. He was dying. He was dying, and when he did, he would stay in Hell for ever and ever and ever.

The Devil's grandmother sat up.

"Grandmother," said the Devil, "say 'cute ivory monkey' again."

"Cute ivory monkey again," she repeated.

The Devil rolled his eyes. "Close enough."

"Hey! Who's that?" she demanded, pointing at Joringel.

"He came to get his sister out of Hell. His plan has gone rather awry, I'm afraid."

"Well, put him down! You don't strangle little boys! It's not nice!" She pulled herself slowly to her feet.

"Grandmother, I'm the Devil. Nice isn't what I *do*."

Joringel began to slip in and out of consciousness.

The Devil's grandmother put her hands on her hips. "Well, you're in my house, you eat my food, and you follow my rules when you're here. Put the little boy down!"

"*Grandmother!*" the Devil whined, his voice lower, "you're *embarrassing* me!"

"Lucifer Satan, I wouldn't care if I was embarrassing you in front of God himself! You listen to your grandmother! We do not strangle little boys in the house!"

"But—"

"Lukey!"

The Devil put the little boy down. Joringel collapsed to his hands and knees, frantically trying to suck air down his crumpled windpipe.

"There, there," the Devil's grandmother said. She lowered her great girth beside the little boy and began to pet him. The Devil's grandmother. Petting Joringel. The Devil watched, disgusted.

"Now, what's all this about your sister? In Hell?"

Joringel, still gasping at the air, tried to nod.

"Was she a much older sister? Was she loose? I bet she was one of those loose girls . . . I was never one of those. You could get me in the back of the car, but you couldn't—"

"She wasn't loose, Grandmother," the Devil cut in, before any details emerged. "She was a tyrant. A bloody-minded oppressor of people."

"What? How old was this sister of yours?"

Joringel managed to gasp, "Twins. We were twins—"

"What? A little girl? A tyrant?" She turned to her grandson. "Lukey, don't exaggerate. You know I don't like that."

"Grandmother, I'm not! She was a tyrant! And this boy here would beat parents in the street!"

"What?" the grandmother looked sternly at Joringel. He was finally sitting up on the floor. His shoulders rose and fell dramatically, and it hurt to breathe, but at least he could draw air into his lungs again. "Why would you do such a thing?"

"They . . . they were abusing their children."

"Oh! Then they deserved it!"

"Grandmother!"

"What? It's true! You don't hit a child. But," she said, turning back to Joringel, "your sister, a tyrant? Was she really?"

Joringel shrugged. "Maybe."

"Why? She was just a little girl . . ."

Joringel didn't know what to say. He thought back to his sister's reign. He couldn't explain it. He couldn't explain why he helped her, either. He had just felt . . . so angry. He told the Devil's grandmother this.

"Angry? About what?"

Joringel shrugged.

"Now don't do that. Talk to Granny. You've got to talk it out."

Joringel looked up into her eyes. They were red. Entirely red, with little black dots for pupils. But, somehow, they looked kind.

"It's a long story."

"Then let's go into the living room and get comfortable."

"I don't know all of it . . . My sister knows the rest."

"Well, then let's go get her!"

"What?" the Devil barked. "Grandmother, no!"

"Lukey . . ." Her voice was stern.

"Grandmother, I can't get a sinner *out* of a Cocoon of Solitude!"

"Why not?"

"Because . . . because it's embarrassing!"

"Lukey . . ."

"Grandmother!"

"Lukey, don't make me raise my voice," the Devil's grandmother said, very quietly.

"It isn't fair!" the Devil pouted. He glared at Joringel. Then he stared at the ceiling. Then he stormed out of the house.

The Devil's grandmother smiled at Joringel. "You just take it easy until he gets back. Then we'll talk this whole thing through, okay?" Joringel nodded. "Would you like a nice, hot cup of tea?"

Joringel squinted. "What kind of tea?"

"Earl Grey's Blood."

"No," said Joringel. "No, thank you."

The Devil's grandmother shrugged and rose to make some for herself.

Joringel waited on the couch made of human scalps, staring at the Devil's front door, waiting for it to open, praying that it would, and that the Devil would come through it with Jorinda (which, he realized, was a strange thing to pray for), hoping against all reasonable hope that she would be okay. In the kitchen, the Devil's grandmother was boiling blood for her tea.

At last, the doorknob turned, the door swung open, and the Devil appeared. A limp body was slung over his shoulder.

"Jorinda?" Joringel cried.

The Devil unslung the little body and dropped it, rather hard, on the floor.

"Is she okay?" Joringel asked, falling to his sister's side.

"She's just been in HELL," the Devil said. "If she *is* okay, I need a new job."

The Devil's grandmother appeared in the doorway of the kitchen. "I'll make her some tea."

"No!" said Joringel. "Thank you. No tea." He bent over his sister. Her face was white and peaceful as a cloud. "Jorinda?" he whispered. "Jorinda? Can you hear me?"

She moaned.

"Jorinda! Jorinda! Wake up!"

Her eyes roved behind her eyelids. "Joringel?"

"I'm here! Wake up! Open your eyes! Please!" Joringel was fighting back tears now. "Please, wake up!"

The Devil turned away. From the kitchen doorway, his grandmother dabbed at her eyes with a handkerchief.

Slowly, Jorinda's eyelids fluttered open. She looked at her

brother. And then there spread across her face a smile so sweet, so pure, so rich with relief that Joringel nearly buckled. He fell upon her. She lifted her thin arms and wrapped them around him. Quietly, they cried.

Joringel murmured, "If you won't leave me, I won't leave you." And Jorinda murmured back, "I will never, ever leave you."

Which, you will be glad to hear, is finally true.

Still, they're both in Hell, so that might not be a good thing.

As the children held each other, the Devil shouted, "This is *disgusting*! It is disgusting, and I will not have it! Not in Hell. Not in my grandmother's house. Stop this instant! Stop! I said stop it!" But Jorinda and Joringel didn't care.

The Devil's grandmother blew her nose into her handkerchief. Then she settled down on the couch and cleared her throat.

The two children turned to her. "Well?" she said. "Tell Granny all about it. And I want *details*."

"She wants to know why you're in Hell," Joringel explained to his sister. "Why you were a tyrant. Why we were both so angry."

Jorinda's eyes, still shining and wet, drifted back and forth between her brother and this red-eyed, orange-haired, buxom old lady sitting on a couch of human scalps.

"I told her it was a long story."

"Which," the Devil's grandmother interjected, "is my favorite kind."

Jorinda's voice was creaky when she said, "Where should we start?"

"Personally," said the Devil's grandmother, "I think the beginning would do very nicely."

The Devil rolled his eyes. "Granny—

"Shhhht! Not a word! The children are talking!"

Jorinda looked helplessly to her brother. Joringel shrugged. Then he smiled. Then he said,

Once upon a time, in the days when fairy tales really happened, there lived a man and his wife. They were a happy couple, for they had everything their hearts desired . . .

"How did your voice get like that?" the Devil demanded.

"Get like what?"

The grandmother and Jorinda were staring at Joringel.

"All loud and bold and boomy!" the Devil said.

"I-I don't know . . ." Joringel stammered.

The Devil's grandmother leaned forward. "Well, don't stop!

It sounds good!"

So Joringel went on. He told of how badly his parents wanted a child and of how his mother had wished for it under the juniper tree after cutting her thumb.

She bore twins: a little boy with dark hair, dark eyes, and lips as red as blood; and a little girl with dark hair and green eyes and cheeks as white as snow.

She brought them to her husband. And this man took one look at his two beautiful children, and he was so happy that he died.

"WHAT?" the grandmother cried. "He was so happy that he *died*?"

Jorinda nodded and cut in. "It happens all the time. It's just . . . 'Oh, I'm so happy! I'm so happy! I'm so ha-a-a-ack-ack-ack . . .'—Dead."

The Devil snickered. His grandmother looked horrified.

Joringel went on with the story. He told of how their mother withdrew from them, how she spent all her time in her study, and how she eventually married their stepfather.

As he told it, Joringel's face became tighter. His shoulders hunched. When he described his mother taking the children into their study, Jorinda looked away. He told about the stone under the mattresses and stamping out the weeds.

"And never cry," Joringel recounted their mother saying. *"Choke back your tears. Tears are waves on the ocean of sadness. You will drown in them if you're not careful. Believe me. I know."*

The grandmother clucked. "That's an awful thing to teach a child! No wonder you're so angry at her!"

Jorinda objected. "We're not angry at *her!*"

The grandmother looked confused. "Oh! Excuse me!"

Joringel went on with the story. After a little while, he came to this part:

I bent down and leaned my head over the apples. They smelled fresh and rich, and their yellow skin was dappled with rose and—

BANG!

Our stepfather slammed the lid of the chest down.

Right on the back of my neck.

And my head fell off into the apples.

"WHAT?" the grandmother screamed.

"THAT'S AWESOME!" cried the Devil.

"Lukey!"

"What, Grandmother? I'm sorry! It is!"

Joringel went on. Soon, he came to this part:

Finally, the man took Jorinda by the shoulders and whispered, "There, there, my dear. Don't cry. Come in the kitchen." And then he added, *"I'll help you hide the body."*

The grandmother, under her breath, whispered, "No . . ."

So our stepfather dragged my body into the kitchen, and Jorinda carried my head, weeping furiously. And then our stepfather took a big knife, and he carved the meat from my bones. And then he threw it into the largest stew pot.

"I LOVE IT!" screamed the Devil.

"Lukey!"

The Devil ignored her. "Is this true? This is the best story I've ever heard!"

"It gets worse," Joringel informed him.

"You mean better?"

"Well, depends on your perspective," Jorinda said. "It definitely gets bloodier."

"Oh, goody!" squealed the Devil.

So Joringel finished his part of the story. And Jorinda started hers.

Once upon a time, I knelt under a juniper tree and tried not to weep . . .

When the stepsisters cut off chunks of their feet, the Devil snickered. "I know them! They're down here now! I know them!"

"Calm down, Lukey."

The two children traded off telling stories all night long.

The Devil cackled when Joringel cut the corpses down from the tree. He clapped his hands when the half man tried to strangle Jorinda, and then chortled when she untied his string. The grandmother gaped at the castle that had fallen asleep and bit her black nails when the huntsman pursued the baby unicorn. And both the grandmother and the Devil smiled knowingly when Joringel told of the ivory monkey.

Finally, they came to the period when Jorinda was queen and Joringel the self-appointed Protector of Children. They described it all as honestly as they could. The grandmother's face became very serious.

"I just felt so . . . so mixed up," Jorinda said.

"When I saw that mother beating her child," Joringel added, "it was like I couldn't see. I felt like I was underwater. Like I was drowning."

"We were angry," Jorinda added. "All the time. I was scared of how angry I was—how angry we were."

"You were angry at your mother," the grandmother concluded matter-of-factly. "You were angry that she neglected you."

"I was not!" Jorinda snapped.

Joringel agreed with his sister.

The grandmother and the Devil both looked surprised.

"You really don't think you were mad at your mother?" the grandmother asked.

"Why would we be mad at her?"

"She was wonderful."

The grandmother raised her eyebrows. "She *neglected* you! She left you alone! All the time! She let that awful man try to murder you! Actually, she let him *succeed* in murdering you!"

"It's not her fault!" Jorinda insisted.

"She was alone!" agreed Joringel.

"She had no one to help her!"

"If she had had help . . ."

"If Father hadn't died . . ."

"If we hadn't *killed* him . . ."

"She would have been a perfect mother."

"We were just too much for her. She couldn't take care of both of us."

Jorinda sighed. "Maybe if we hadn't been so much work . . ."

Joringel nodded. "Or if Father had still been alive . . ."

The Devil and his grandmother both sat there on the couch made of human scalps, dumbstruck.

"Wait," said the Devil, "are you blaming *yourselves*?"

"Were you listening?" his grandmother responded. "Of course they're blaming themselves."

ADAM GIDWITZ

"But—but," stammered the Devil, "that's ridiculous!"

"Of *course* it's ridiculous!" his grandmother replied. "Of all the conclusions to draw from that long, bloody, horrible, grim story we just heard, that is the *most* ridiculous conclusion you could possibly come up with."

"I don't think it's so ridiculous," Jorinda said, so quietly her voice was almost just breath.

"We killed our father," Joringel whispered.

"You *killed* your father? You *killed* your father?" the Devil's grandmother cried. "How, exactly, did you do that? You were born? You answered your parents' dearest wish and were born? And were beautiful? That's your crime? Your father didn't die of happiness! He died from a heart attack! Or a brain aneurysm! Or high cholesterol!"

Jorinda and Joringel stared.

"And your mother," she went on, "your poor, heartsick mother, *abandoned* you in her own home! This is your fault? Because she can't be a grown-up about losing her husband? *This* is your fault?"

The children said nothing.

"What else? What else do you blame yourselves for?"

Jorinda swallowed hard. "For leaving Joringel."

Joringel's heart caught in his throat.

"You were going to marry a prince!" the grandmother shouted at Jorinda. "And you?" she asked, turning to Joringel.

"Had Jorinda loved me more, she wouldn't have left," Joringel said quietly.

Jorinda made a sound in her throat like she was choking.

"She—was—going—to—marry—a—prince!" the grandmother cried. "When that opportunity comes, you take it!"

The Devil nodded. His voice was a little shaky when he said, "She's right, you know."

The children stared at the Devil and his grandmother.

"It isn't your fault," the grandmother said. "Either one of you. None of this. You have been brave. You have been loving. Occasionally, you have been a little bit stupid. But who isn't? None of this is your fault. Can you see that now?"

Tears slowly made their way over the children's cheeks. They shrugged. But Jorinda smiled. Joringel half laughed.

"It was kind of silly," Joringel said through a crooked grin, sniffling. "We were just born."

"Yeah," agreed Jorinda. "That's all we did. And I wanted to marry a prince. That's not so bad."

"Not so bad at all," Joringel said. "Not so bad at all." He sighed a deep, rattling sigh.

Suddenly, the Devil drew his sleeve savagely across his face. "OKAY!" he bellowed, standing up. "That's enough!"

His grandmother and the two children both shrank before him.

The Devil towered over them, his great red shoulders rising and falling. "You will not—I repeat, will NOT—make me cry in my own home! Get out! Get OUT, and never, ever come back!"

Jorinda and Joringel smiled.

"NOW!" he roared.

The children leaped to their feet.

"Will you take any leftovers?" the Devil's grandmother asked. "There's more brisket!"

The children shook their heads vigorously.

"NOW!" the Devil exploded. And then, without any warning, he buried his face in his sleeve, ran into the back of the house, and slammed the door to his room. Even with his door closed, they could all hear him crying into a pillow.

His grandmother smiled, led the children to the door, and said, "The exit's that way." She kissed them roughly on their foreheads, leaving great black lipstick marks just below their hairlines. "Now do what my grandson says," she told them, "and never come back."

And they never did.

The Ruined Land

Once upon a time, there was a very grim kingdom.

Up and down Grimm's brown, barren fields, the soldiers marched, chanting to the dusty skies, "Protect our king! Protect our king!"

Rumors ran through the inns and public spaces. It was said that Joringel would return, looking for revenge. That he would bring an army with him that would dwarf any army Grimm had ever seen. That when he arrived, parents would be executed and children would rule over the land. Fear your children, the rumors said. For when Joringel comes, they will rise from their beds, knives clutched in their tiny hands, do you in, and then rush out to join the tyrant.

New laws had been introduced. Children were not allowed out of their houses alone. Any children on the streets had to be attached to an adult by rope or chain. Children found alone out of doors were to be arrested. Children who fled were to be killed.

Some parents went easy on their young ones: they obeyed the law, for fear of the soldiers, but treated their young ones with secret kindness. But others needed very little convincing to fear their children. They chained them to posts and beat them in the streets for the least infraction. They locked them in basements at night, to prevent their escape. They cursed them. They neglected them.

It was a very grim kingdom indeed.

I know what you're thinking. You're thinking, How, how could the prince do all this? He seemed like such a nice boy! Maybe a little stupid. Well, maybe incredibly stupid. But not cruel. Not like this.

Right you are. The prince, stupid and self-centered as he was, was no tyrant.

No. Captain Herzlos, of the scarred face and long, black hair, was the tyrant.

For the cunning captain had whipped the subjects of Grimm on Jorinda's behalf. He had betrayed the castle into the prince's hands. He had murdered her in the Kingswood. And finally he had locked the weak-willed prince in his room—with only his colored blocks to play with. For the good of the kingdom, Herzlos said.

Now the ruthless and efficient King Herzlos sat on the throne of Grimm.

He was the cruelest tyrant the land had ever known.

Jorinda and Joringel traveled a dusty road into the kingdom. On either side of them lay dead fields, tramped into submission by a thousand boots. Widowed houses with black, empty windows peered over the once green farms. A goat's skull, half buried in the loose dirt, smiled at them as flies seethed over what little flesh remained. The whole kingdom rotted—field after field, house after house, goat's skull after goat's skull.

(Okay, there was only one goat's skull.)

"Who did this?" Joringel asked, bewildered. "Who sacked the farms? Who ruined the land?"

Jorinda sighed. "We did, Little Brother. We did."

Joringel hung his head.

—

It was true. After all, Herzlos had only continued what Jorinda and Joringel had begun.

As Jorinda and Joringel got closer to the center of the kingdom, fewer houses were abandoned. A few shops were open. They saw people on the road. One noticed them and stared. Jorinda and Joringel, for fear of being recognized, slid into the shadow of an abandoned home. There, they rubbed dirt on their faces and into their tattered clothes.

When they emerged from behind the house, their eyes fell upon a small girl with black hair and a spray of freckles across her nose. She was crouched in the dirt, peeling potatoes with a dull blade. The rinds fell into a small, cracked bowl. The potatoes she threw in a pot.

The little girl looked up to see Jorinda and Joringel emerging from the shadows, and she gasped. Her knife slipped, cutting her thumb. Red blood fell to the dusty ground. "Ow!" she cried.

"Eva! What'd you do?" bellowed a voice from inside.

The little girl's eyes were wide and frightened. Not of the voice, though. Of Jorinda and Joringel. "What . . . where are your chains?" she whispered.

Jorinda and Joringel were confused.

The little girl motioned down at their ankles. Then she stood up. A shackle was buckled around her little heel, and to the shackle was clamped a heavy iron chain.

Jorinda demanded, "Why are you chained like a dog?"

The little girl didn't know how to answer her.

"Eva!" a woman's voice bellowed. It was coming closer.

"You should run," said the little girl, glancing behind her. "If my mother sees you, she'll call for the soldiers. She's on their side."

"On whose side?" Joringel asked.

"The king's! The adults'!"

"EVA!" Suddenly, the little girl's feet were jerked out from under her and her chin slammed into the bowl of potato skins, breaking it in three. Jorinda fell to the girl's side.

"Hey! Who are you? Where are your parents?" a voice bellowed. Standing in the doorway of the house was a round woman with a red face and oily red hair. In her hands, she held the other end of the little girl's chain. She yanked it again. Eva slid back toward her house, leaving two trails of blood in the dirt—one from her thumb, and the other from her chin. The fat woman's beady eyes did not leave Jorinda or Joringel. "Where are your chains?"

Jorinda and Joringel stared, uncomprehending.

"SOLDIERS! HELP! SOLDIERS! CHILDREN ON THE LOOSE!" the woman's sharp, nasal voice rattled the windowpanes in the nearby houses. Doors flew open. Shutters clattered and heads emerged. "CHILDREN! CHILDREN!"

Little Eva gazed up desperately at Jorinda and Joringel. "Go!" she whispered. "*Go!*"

They ran behind the abandoned house, sprinted down the dusty roadway, and then crawled through a barren field until they could no longer hear the people shouting. At the edge of the field they found a broken-down toolshed. They pushed in the rickety wooden slats of the door and crawled into the darkness.

"What was that?" Jorinda asked.

"No idea." Joringel heaved.

"What is going on?"

Joringel shook his head.

The children sat in the damp cool of the shed until their breath returned to normal.

"We should figure it out," Jorinda announced.

"I think, maybe, we should just leave," said Joringel.

"It's our kingdom."

"It *used* to be our kingdom."

"This is all our fault."

"It isn't." Joringel's face was scrunched up. "We didn't ask to be born, remember?"

But Jorinda replied, "Just because *that* isn't our fault doesn't mean nothing is." She gestured at the ruined field through the broken slats of the shed. "*This* is our fault."

Joringel didn't speak for a moment. They could hear the wind eddying over the dusty field. The little shed creaked.

"I don't want to walk away again," Jorinda whispered. Her words hung in the damp darkness.

Joringel sighed. At last, he said, "Then there's only one place to go."

Jorinda nodded. The dusk collected over the barren field. "But not now," she said.

"No?"

"No. Tomorrow." Jorinda drew her shirt tight around her and dropped her head onto her brother's shoulder. "Tomorrow, we can go home."

Dear Reader,

I have some advice for you. And, being much older than you (probably), and much wiser than you (just take my word for it), I recommend that you listen to it.

If you are trying to keep all your feelings smothered down and stamped out and choked back—and I'm not saying you should, I'm just saying maybe you are—do not do what Jorinda and Joringel are about to do.

Do not go home.

If you have a stone that you have smothered under mattresses, and you hope to keep it smothered, do not go home. If you have weeds that you have stamped upon and stamped upon until they withered and died, and you want them to stay dead, do not go home. If you have tears locked inside your stomach, churning around like some tempestuous inland sea, and you cannot bear to let them out, do not go home.

For home is the quarry that the stone was cut from. Home is the wild field that blew the weeds into your yard. Home is the wellspring of all your salty tears.

Two children stood beneath a juniper tree.

The sky was inky and full of stars, but the horizon was a smudge of cream-like gray with hints of blue. Above their heads, in the fragrant, piney juniper branches, a little bird announced that the morning was near. The little house in which Jorinda and Joringel had grown up was dark.

And then a candle flickered to life in a windowpane on the first floor. The scene suddenly looked like a painting: one window, a rectangle of buttery yellow, framed by the gray and black landscape. Jorinda reached out and took her brother's hand.

"She's awake," the little girl whispered. Still, the children stood there, like deer at the edge of a strange field—tense and alert. They had not come home once since the day they had left. Though they lived in Grimm for a year and more—in the castle, no less—they had never done it. And their mother, closed as she was in her study every morning and every evening, had never come looking for them, either.

Finally, the children took hands and crossed the space between the juniper tree and the door to their childhood home. The grass was sodden with dew. The little bird in the juniper tree raised its voice so the whole countryside could hear. The stars overhead were fading.

Jorinda was the one to open the front door—unlocked, of course. For who, now that their mother lived alone, would remember to lock it? Joringel led the way through the foyer—where he had sat, long ago, his head unnaturally leaning to one side, his face pale, his eyes wide, a handkerchief reddening around his neck, an apple in his hand.

The door to her study was closed. A bar of guttering light crawled out from beneath it.

Jorinda glanced at her brother. His jaw was moving side to side in his head. She raised her eyebrows. He nodded. Jorinda reached out her hand and knocked a hollow knock on the old pine door.

The children waited. There was the dull thud of a book being dropped to the floor. Pages rustled like dead leaves in autumn. The seconds crawled by.

At last, the door swung open, and Jorinda and Joringel saw their mother, blinking at them through her reading glasses, her limp brown hair folded up in a messy bun.

For one second, no one spoke. They just stood there.

Then their mother said, "Hold on. I'm at an important part. I'll be right out." She pushed the door of the study closed.

Jorinda and Joringel stared at the worn wood of the pine door. They knew every knot in it, every whorl. Closed. Just as it had always been.

And then, very slowly, it opened. Their mother leaned against the old, warped wood. A crooked smile jagged its way across her face. Her eyes were bright with tears.

"Sorry," she said. "That was my poor idea of a joke."

And then she reached out and pulled her children to her and wrapped her arms around them, and as they held her, Jorinda and Joringel inhaled the scent of their mother. After a minute,

284   ADAM GIDWITZ

Jorinda and Joringel tried to pull away. But their mother would not release them. They laughed—and then their eyes brimmed, and overflowed. Slowly, the sky began to brighten in the study window. Streaks of pink illuminated the morning. The minutes passed. And the tears continued to course through their lashes, fluently, endlessly, as if all the water that had ever sloshed around in the children's stomachs was now pouring from their eyes—and still their mother clutched them. And she whispered, "Thank you. Thank you. Thank you for coming home."

The kitchen clattered with plates and forks and pans and glassware. Eggs sizzled in butter, and a loaf of bread browned in the oven, lacing the air with its yeasty scent. The children ate hungrily. Their mother watched them, grinning like a fool.

After breakfast, the morning was bright and warm. Jorinda and Joringel went out and sat with their mother beneath the juniper tree and watched a doe rabbit nose her kittens across the short grass, nibbling clover. The children were exhausted, but they were happy to lean their heads against their mother's soft shoulders and stare across the distant rolling fields.

"Do you know," their mother murmured, "that it hurts me to look at you?"

Jorinda pulled herself slowly away from her mother and peered up into those tired, misty eyes. "It does?"

Their mother nodded.

"Because you're still angry at us?" Joringel asked.

A shadow crossed their mother's face. "Angry at you? When was I angry at you?"

Joringel shrugged and looked to his sister. Jorinda said, "Because of what happened to Father."

Their mother still did not understand.

Joringel said, "He died when we were born."

Their mother seemed to fold in on herself. Her face grayed, sagged. She whispered, "I was never angry at you. I'm sorry you thought that. You are the most miraculous children I could ever have imagined. No, it hurts to look at you because I love you *so much*." She gazed at the window of her study, reflecting the warm light of the mid-morning sun. "I spent so much time away from you not because I was angry, but because I was trying not to be afraid. Afraid of how much I loved you, afraid of how miraculous you both were, afraid that I would not be a good enough mother for you. I was trying to shut out my fear. To shove it down. To forget about it."

"To cover it with mattresses," Jorinda said.

"To stamp out the weeds," Joringel added.

"To choke back the tears," Jorinda concluded.

Their mother winced. "Where did you learn that?"

"You, Mama," Jorinda said.

Their mother sighed sharply. "No matter how many mattresses I threw on that stone, I still felt it."

The children stared up at their mother, watching her think.

"No matter how I stamped on the weeds, they still grew back." She paused. "And I killed the good plants, too."

The children waited, not breathing.

"Choking back the tears just felt like choking."

The children smiled sadly.

"Will you forgive me for being so stupid?" their mother asked them. They laughed. But the mother folded her children in her arms again and held them—held them as tightly as she had always wanted to.

Okay, I suppose there is one benefit to going home.

It's true that home is the quarry, the wild field, and the wellspring.

But until you plumb the quarry, you will not know its depths; until you run through the field, you will not bask in its sunshine; until you bathe at the source of the tears, you will never be clean.

Then, from the road that led toward their house, they heard the stamping of feet. It came in unison, like distant drums. A cloud of dust billowed over the hill.

"Quick!" their mother said. "Get inside!"

Jorinda and Joringel were on their feet in a flash, across the green yard, and into their little house. Their mother followed close behind.

"Soldiers," she said, watching at the window.

"Are they coming here?" Jorinda demanded.

After a silent minute, her mother said, "No. Just passing."

Jorinda exhaled.

"Mama, we saw the strangest thing," Joringel said. "A little girl had a chain around her ankle, like she was a wild beast. She seemed surprised that we didn't have one."

"The new laws," she said. She moved the children away from the windows. They sat down at the kitchen table, and she explained the new laws to Jorinda and Joringel. The children listened in horror.

"The prince did all this?" Jorinda asked, incredulous.

"Not the prince. The new king. Herzlos." And their mother described how Herzlos had imprisoned the prince—for the good of the kingdom, supposedly—and taken the throne himself.

Jorinda, Joringel, and their mother sat in the kitchen, looking at their hands.

"We have to do something," Jorinda announced. "This is my fault."

"Our fault," Joringel corrected her. "The laws against bad parents were my idea." After a moment, he said, "I could just turn myself in. Then they wouldn't be afraid of me coming back to rally the children and rebel. This might all end."

Jorinda shook her head. "You don't believe that. It wouldn't end."

"No," said their mother. "It wouldn't."

"We need to free the children," Joringel asserted.

"They need a safe place to go," said Jorinda.

"Okay," Joringel said. "Let's find a safe place for them to go. Then we free them."

Their mother smiled sadly. "My dears, you'd surely be caught. And even if you did free them, would they come with you? Where would they go?"

"What about the forest next to Malchizedek's house?" Jorinda suggested. "No one ever goes out there."

Joringel nodded vigorously. "We could all live out in the woods, there by the quarry!"

"It would be like a kingdom!" Jorinda agreed, warming to the idea. "A kingdom of children."

Joringel repeated that. "The Kingdom of Children. I like the sound of that."

Their mother was looking at Jorinda and Joringel wistfully. "Let's not get carried away, my dears. This is a very sweet idea, but it isn't realistic. We've got to get you two away from here as soon as we can. Freeing the other children won't be possible."

Jorinda and Joringel bowed their heads. The kitchen was heavy with silence.

Jorinda stood up from the kitchen table. "Mother, have you ever ruled a kingdom?"

Her mother blinked up at her. "Well, no . . ."

Joringel stood up beside his sister. "Have you rescued a castle from an eternal sleep?"

"Of course not, but . . ."

"Have you survived a corpse trying to choke you to death?"

"What?!"

"Or scaled the walls of a castle at night?"

Their mother gaped.

"Have you ridden a unicorn?"

"Or turned into a bird?"

"Have you gone to Hell?"

"And come back alive?"

The mother stared wonderingly at her two children. "You . . . you did all that?"

Jorinda and Joringel nodded solemnly.

A smile of awe spread across their mother's face.

"Okay," she said slowly. "Okay. Let's get started."

The Kingdom
of Children

O nce upon a time, two children owned the night. They slithered through fields. They tapped at windows. They whispered under doors. They led sleepy and bewildered kids out of their houses and into a redwood forest.

At dawn the next morning, twelve dazed children sat around a little fire under towering pines. Soft ferns grew up from the pine needles that lined the ground. Birds dove and zipped between the enormous trees. The twins' mother prepared warm milk in a pot over a fire. She served it in cracked mugs to each of the shivering children. Jorinda and Joringel stood, surveying their work.

"How many kids are there in Grimm?" Joringel asked.

"I think about a thousand," Jorinda replied.

"How many do we have here?"

"Twelve."

Joringel scratched his head. "Huh. Not quite a majority."

"No."

"How are we going to get the rest?"

Jorinda crouched before the other children. "Two kids freed twelve," she said. "Now we're fourteen. So fourteen could free . . ."

Across the fire, a small boy's eyes lit up. "Eighty-four!" he cried.

"Wow!" Jorinda exclaimed. "That was impressive."

The boy was missing his two front teeth. He spoke very quickly. "You just assume a constant rate of six children per rescuer, and then you multiply—"

Joringel interrupted him. "How many kids could eighty-four free?"

"It'd be ninety-eight, including us," the gap-toothed boy reported. "And ninety-eight could free five hundred and eighty-eight!"

"So in three days, we could have all the kids in Grimm here," Jorinda said.

"Easily!"

"Not easily," their mother objected, pouring more milk into

a child's cup. "But it is, theoretically, possible."

A little girl with curly black hair and freckles and a cut on her chin stood up. "What are we going to do out here? Once they're all freed?"

"We're going to start our own kingdom. A kingdom of children," Jorinda replied.

A smile slowly stretched across little Eva's face. "Then we'll help."

Their calculations were wrong. Fourteen children did not free eighty-four. They freed a hundred and fifty-eight—for each pair focused on their friends and relatives, who needed far less convincing than strangers did. And, the next night, in one of the most astounding covert operations since the horse at Troy, a hundred and fifty-eight kids, plus the original fourteen, guided every remaining child in Grimm—all nine hundred seventy-seven of them—to the red-wooded forest on the farthest edge of the kingdom. There, before an enormous bonfire of pine needles and fallen branches, the entire population of Grimm between the ages of four and sixteen spread out on the ground (they'd had to leave the toddlers—for sake of speed and stealth; toddlers aren't very good at either). The children talked animatedly, finding friends and hugging them, rubbing their ankles or their wrists where the shackles had dug into their skin.

Jorinda climbed up onto an enormous fallen log. "Attention!" she cried. She was inaudible over the thrum of a thousand children's voices. "ATTENTION!" she cried again. No good.

"Shhhhhhhhh . . ." Joringel whispered. Children love nothing more than to shush other children. So the syllable was taken up first by those in the front, and then spread, like a blanket, all the way to the rear of the group. But then the children took to shushing the shushes, until a veritable shush-war had broken out. Jorinda put her hands on her hips. "This is going to be harder than I thought," she whispered. "Adults are much better at following directions than kids."

"That's why adults stink," Joringel replied.

Their mother, sitting beside them on the large log, said, "May I?"

Her children shrugged.

She stood up beside them. The children of Grimm continued to shush each other lustily.

Very quietly, she said, "The first one who's quiet gets cake." The shushes died away.

Jorinda's mouth hung open. "Thanks," she muttered.

Her mother nodded and got down, muttering, "Now I've got to find some cake . . ."

Jorinda gazed out over the thousand-plus heads staring

298   ADAM GIDWITZ

back at her through the night. She took a deep breath, and then bellowed, "I AM JORINDA."

A wave of whispers rushed through the group. "You're dead!" someone shouted.

"Clearly, I'm not!" Jorinda cried.

Children leaned forward, straining their eyes against the darkness to see the little girl who stood in the dancing light of the great fire.

"The king lied to you!" she shouted. (He hadn't, of course, lied to them. She had indeed been dead. But that was too hard to explain right now.) "I have returned! With Joringel!" She gripped her brother's hand and raised it.

Disbelief gave way to a sudden wave of tension. The children's faces no longer looked happy and free. They were concerned. Was this not what the adults had predicted? Was this not the reason for the laws in the first place? The children began to shift uncomfortably.

"We are not here to rule over you again," Jorinda announced.

Strained murmurs echoed in the firelit night.

"We were really bad at that."

Some of the children chuckled. Others murmured.

"Terrible."

More chuckles than murmurs.

"Joringel and I have brought you here to free you. To resist the rule of the king. To start a kingdom of no kings or queens at all. To create a kingdom of children."

In all the dark pine forest, there was not a single sound save the hot roar of the bonfire and the breaking of pine needles under hundreds of shifting, nervous children.

"Some of you will watch while some sleep. Some will gather food and cook while some care for the smaller ones. We will stay here as long as we have to. As long as the adults are crazy."

Murmurs and scattered laughter.

"What if they find us?" someone cried out. "What if they send the soldiers to get us?"

"We will build a fortress!" Joringel cut in. "We will defend ourselves!"

"We are just children!" the voice cried.

The forest grew deathly still. They were, indeed, just children.

But then Jorinda said, "There is a power in children. There is a belief. A strength. A joy that makes just about anything possible."

I don't know if you know it, dear reader. But this, without any doubt, is true.

Indeed, something hummed among the children of Grimm. No one said a word, and yet there it was. Belief. Strength. Excitement. Joy. Humming and thrumming through the darkness.

"Will you stay?"

Some heads nodded. Many hesitated.

"Will you?" Joringel cried.

And some children, quietly, said, "Yes."

"Will you?" Jorinda cried.

And now some children shouted, "Yes!"

"Will you?" Joringel cried.

More answered, "Yes!"

"WILL YOU?" they both shouted together. And the children realized that they were being called, they were being trusted, they were being freed—freed to free themselves. It would be up to them. Together. To free themselves, and their brothers, and their sisters, and their friends.

And a roar answered Jorinda and Joringel. A roar of yes.

And so began perhaps the most amazing few weeks in the history of the Kingdom of Grimm. Out there in the forest, on the edge of the granite quarry, a thousand children began to build a life for themselves.

On the first day, Jorinda and Joringel assigned tasks. Every child was divided into one of two groups, Seekers and Makers. The Seekers were the small, swift, crafty children. They were to sneak back into the towns and houses they'd come from and steal as much as they could. No money, of course, for that was no good in the forest. Only food and blankets, tools and weapons.

Yes. Weapons. For Jorinda and Joringel did not know when the adults would find them. But they would. And when they did, they would be angry. And, perhaps, violent.

The Makers stayed in camp. They prepared the food and gathered moss for beds and built canopies of leaves and branches for when it rained.

Jorinda and Joringel's mother had never been much of a mother at home. But here, under the towering red cedars, she watched over the littlest ones, hustling them from here to there, telling them stories, feeding them when they were hungry, comforting them when they grew homesick. Jorinda and Joringel watched her and felt a strange mixture of emotions that they could not describe. Still, they were grateful to her.

Finally, under the direct supervision of Joringel and a small boy who lacked his two front teeth, the largest, strongest, most inventive Makers built an earthworks and stockade.

Half a mile from the clearing where the children would sleep, these Makers took stolen axes and began to cut down a ring of great red pine trees. They stacked them to one side, and then, around the roots of their stumps they dug with stolen shovels, until they had piled up earth twelve feet high. They moved in a wide semicircle, directed by the brilliant little boy with a mind for figures and shapes. Each day, they strained against the heat and the soft red wood and the hard red dirt. Each day, the earthwork grew a hundred feet or more in length as two hundred strong boys and girls chopped and heaved and dug and heaved some more. Each night, they returned to camp covered in red dirt, stinking with sweat, smiling widely. At last, the earthwork stretched in a wide band between a ravine that ran down into the quarry on the right side of the forest, and a deep and swift river a quarter mile distant. Then the children hewed the ends of the felled trees into sharp points. Finally, they buried them deep in the earthwork and lashed them together with ropes.

Each night, the children would gather before the cliff that overlooked the quarry, and by the light of the raging bonfire, the children would sing, or teach each other games, or tell stories. And they were happy.

———

And if this seems strange to you—that, under these difficult, frightening, and outlandish circumstances, children might be happy . . . well, then you don't know all that much about children.

On the twentieth day since the children had arrived in the forest, the wall and earthwork were complete. Jorinda and Joringel gathered all the Seekers and all the Makers before it, and there was much whooping and laughing and pointing and marveling. The little boy with the gap in his teeth strutted back and forth like a rooster before the structure, grinning comically. As much as sixty feet high in places, six feet thick all around, and a quarter mile long, this was not just a wall. The children had built a fortress. And, in the process, a kingdom.

That was the twentieth day.

On the twenty-first day, the soldiers arrived.

It is hard to hide a wall that size. It is also hard to hide a thousand children. Perhaps it was a woodcutter, come out to gather fardels. Perhaps it was a hunter, chasing game. Perhaps it was truffle farmer, loosing his pigs among the roots.

Whoever it was, someone saw the great wall in the midst

of the forest. The stockade that had not been there before. The fortress that had just appeared. That person told someone else, who told someone else. Word soon reached King Herzlos.

The morning on the twenty-first day was clear, and cool. Birds sang and chattered in the swaying trees, and the fallen pine needles swept across the dry red earth like the straw of a broom.

It was not the sort of day one would expect so many people to die.

Up the long red road that led from the Castle Grimm to that forest along the quarry came a company of soldiers. The steel tips of their spears flashed in the rising sun, and the dull iron of their helmets rose and fell like an undulating metal quilt.

From the top of the fortress wall, a cry was raised. Jorinda and Joringel were called, and they came, clambering up the ladder to the small platform that served as a lookout.

"Here they come," Jorinda whispered. She turned. Little Eva waited at the bottom of the ladder. "This is it," Jorinda told her. "Get 'em ready."

Joringel was peering into the distance. "It isn't many. Maybe a hundred."

Jorinda pursed her lips. "There's more coming. Trust me."

Indeed, another company of soldiers followed the first. In the distance, the children could hear the drums that accompanied the army as it marched.

"Now I see three groups of soldiers," Joringel said, straining his eyes through the blue morning haze.

Jorinda said, "And I'll bet you there's a fourth behind that one. And a fifth behind that. And a sixth behind that."

Joringel asked, "How many soldiers do you think Herzlos would send?"

"Well, I think the army of Grimm has about three thousand men and women."

"Right . . ." said Joringel.

"So I'd expect about three thousand."

Joringel murmured, "They wouldn't—"

Eva's head poked up onto the platform. She had climbed a ladder that lay against the stockade. "Three thousand what?" she asked.

"Soldiers," answered Jorinda. "Is everyone set?"

Eva nodded. Jorinda and Joringel turned and surveyed their force. They were arrayed behind the wall. The little boy with the gap in his teeth ran back and forth, barking orders at the bigger children. Jorinda and Joringel's mother stood near the cliff overlooking the quarry with bandages and buckets of warm water.

Little Eva had clambered up onto the platform. Her chin was resting between two sharp points of the stockade. She gazed

ADAM GIDWITZ

out at the approaching army. Very quietly, she asked, "Are we going to die?"

Joringel turned to her. "I don't think so, Eva. I don't think so."

Suddenly, Jorinda was shouting, "At arms! At ARMS!"

A thousand children gripped makeshift shields with one hand—broken chairs, or, between a few children, tables and even the wooden tops of wells—and in the other, each lifted a weapon. There were a few swords, a few spears, but mostly there were kitchen knives and shovels and broomsticks.

"My friends!" Jorinda cried. "Listen now!"

The children's frightened, determined eyes were on Jorinda. Weapons shifted, sweaty hands gripped the handles of the makeshift shields. No other sound was made.

"We have lived here for three weeks. We have lived with no parents. No kings or queens. No adults at all, save one. And we did pretty well, didn't we?"

Some of the children cheered. Others raised their weapons high.

"We journeyed into the wood to escape the prisons of our lives, and here we built and grew and learned. We have made lives here, in the forest. It's the oldest story: A child flees his broken home. He comes to the forest, where he faces his gravest fears and realizes his greatest hopes. But always there comes a time to leave. When the child must take what he has learned in the wood and return to that broken home. To mend it. To save it."

The army of children was silent. Trees creaked in the gentle wind.

"Today, if we triumph, may be that day. Today, if we resist, if we succeed, if we survive, the adults might see how they have hurt us. How they have betrayed us. How they have neglected us. We may win without shedding a drop of blood. That, anyway, is the plan."

Behind Jorinda, the sound of marching grew louder. The sky overhead was clear and blue.

"So stand firm! Stick to the plan! And—"

"JORINGEL!"

The shout came from the other side of the wall.

"JORINGEL!"

Jorinda and Joringel turned. There, before the wall, Herzlos sat astride an enormous black steed. The scars on his face looked dark and deep with fury. He looked up and saw, above the sharp points of the stockade, two heads: Joringel's and Jorinda's.

Herzlos started. "How—" he stammered. "How are you still alive?"

Behind him was arrayed a line of a hundred men. Behind that was another line, and another, and another, ten deep. And behind that, more divisions marched into the forest.

"Oh, who cares?" he snapped. "SURRENDER!"

Jorinda spat back, "We won't!"

Herzlos gritted his teeth and smiled. "I have assembled the greatest military force in the history of Grimm."

"And you would use it to attack children?" Jorinda asked.

Herzlos smiled. "Oh, I will."

"And your soldiers?" Joringel demanded.

Herzlos's face was grim. "They will do as I tell them. Surrender now!"

And Jorinda cried back, "Never!"

Behind her, a thousand children roared. It was an eerie sound, the roar of children. High and fierce and wild. The soldiers shivered.

"Then you will be taken," Herzlos bellowed up at the walls. "Alive or dead." His eyes narrowed. "Preferably the latter."

Jorinda and Joringel both swallowed hard.

Sorry. I need to say something.

In my first book, *A Tale Dark & Grimm*, there was a battle scene. Many people enjoyed it. But some did not. One person in particular did not. My wife.

I told her, "I can't help it! There *was* a great battle! What do you want me to do? Summarize it?"

Well, she told me she wasn't happy about it, but if I was *sure* that was *really* how the story went, she guessed she would deal with it.

Well, I am back to apologize to her. And to you, dear reader, if you happen to find battles upsetting and gratuitous. If you'd like, you can skip right to where the children have been bloodied and the battle is lost. It's on page 320.

As for the rest of you—enjoy, if you can . . .

"Soldiers of Grimm! READY!" Herzlos screamed.

The second and third rows of soldiers drew bows from their backs and nocked arrows in their bowstrings.

Jorinda's face went pale.

"AIM!"

"They wouldn't," Joringel whispered. "Would they fire on children?"

"LOOSE!"

Jorinda and Joringel ducked, and Eva screamed to the children inside the fort, "ARROWS!"

Two hundred arrows drew a high arc over the children's fortifications. Some got lost in the foliage above. But most found a clear path, peaked just above Jorinda's and Joringel's heads, and then began to dive directly for the assembled children.

"COVER!" Eva screamed, and hundreds of makeshift

shields rose to create a solid wall of wood above the children's heads. Arrows hit the wood with thuds and plunks, and fell away, harmless. Except for one. One arrow found a small hole between two children's shields, and buried itself in a small girl's thigh.

Her shriek pierced the forest. Jorinda and Joringel scanned their force for her, and found her, gripping her leg and wailing. Their mother pushed through the children, bringing the bandages and warm water. Joringel turned and peered over the wall just in time to see the captain raise his arm and cry "LOOSE!" And a second batch of arrows were loosed over fortifications.

"COVER!" Eva screamed again, and shields were gripped. *Plunk plunk thunk.* Screams. A large boy had moved to help the little girl, and in so doing had dropped his shield. Now an arrow was lodged in his neck, and the children around him were screaming to see blood burbling up over his shirt.

"LOOSE!"

"COVER!"

The arrows rose, found the gap between the high fortress wall and the foliage above, and fell upon the children. *Plunk plunk plunk.* The shields held.

Jorinda cried, "Courage!"

"They're coming!" Joringel shouted.

Jorinda spun and looked over the wall. The first row of soldiers was running right for them. They crossed the space in an instant, buried their feet in the high, red earthwork, and threw themselves onto the wall.

The soldiers climbed a foot or two up the slick, shorn tree trunks before sliding back down again. The logs of the wall were tightly lashed together at the top, leaving no gaps for footholds or handholds. Soldiers fell, ran at the wall again, leaped onto it, and then pathetically slid to the bottom again, like cats trying to climb a window. Jorinda cocked a crooked smile at Joringel.

But then Herzlos bellowed, "LADDERS! LOOSE!" And as another brace of arrows flew over the wall and Eva screamed, "COVER," forty men ran forward with twenty huge ladders and laid them against the wooden wall.

"CLIMB!" the captain commanded. And the men started to climb the ladders.

"Incoming, Eva," Joringel said, and Eva turned and screamed, "INCOMING!"

Joringel said to Jorinda, "I wish we could just push the ladders off." But they could not. The platform only stood at one narrow place in the wall, and the ladders were far from it.

Jorinda said, "We're ready."

On the ground within the fort, a hundred children surged forward in pairs. One of each pair carried a shield. The other carried a sack. Eva directed the pairs to where the ladders were, while the little boy with the missing teeth watched from the shadow of the wall. The children waited.

When the first soldier climbed to the top of the wall and peered over the sharpened tree trunks, he was met with a rock directly in his face. It struck him in the temple, and he fell from the ladder and landed in a heap at the base of the wall. He did not move.

"Direct hit!" the little boy shouted. The children cheered. Those with the sacks drew out more rocks, while the children with the shields waited, lest another volley of arrows come over the wall.

Two more faces emerged above the stockade. *Smack smack smack.* Three stones were loosed at the two faces, and all three were thrown true. The two soldiers were both knocked off their ladders and fell to the ground, and the children could hear the snap of breaking bones. Another face emerged. Two stones were thrown at him, but the first missed, and the second glanced off his iron helmet. The soldier quickly threw his leg over the wall and leaped to the earth inside the fortress.

"INSIDE! INSIDE!" Eva screamed.

Jorinda and Joringel watched as ten of their largest boys and girls ran to the intruder. The soldier seemed to have hurt his leg leaping down from the wall. The children ran at him with clubs and swords and shovels and then pummeled him—while two kids with spears watched from a few feet off—until he was still. Two more soldiers were knocked off the wall, and one more made it inside, and another team of ten ran forward and beat him senseless.

Way up in a red pine sat three black forms. Birds, actually. Ravens, to be precise.

"Not bad! Not bad!" shouted the first raven.

"Not bad? Incredible!" cried the second.

"Kill him!" screamed the third, as the children pummeled the soldier. "Beat his brains in! Break his arms! Shatter his legs! Cut off his—"

"That's enough," said the first raven curtly.

Down below, Herzlos glowered at the fortifications as his men went toppling off of ladders or disappeared over the wall, never to be seen again. No one opened the gate, as they were instructed to do. There were no screams of frightened children. Nor of dying children. Dying children would have been all right with Herzlos, too. He ground his teeth in his head and barked curses at his men.

Inside the fortress, five men had made it over the wall, and the children were struggling to subdue them all at once. One of the soldiers had evaded the band of ten sent at him and had run right into the middle of the army of children.

"HOLD FAST!" Joringel bellowed at them. And, for the most part, they did. They used their weapons to bludgeon him from all sides. He struck back with the butt of his spear, reluctant to kill. Eventually, the children beat him to the ground.

"Hooray!" Joringel cried.

The battle continued like this. Five, ten, even twenty men at a time made it over the wall, only to be beaten into submission by a thousand children. Jorinda and Joringel's mother, aided by a few older kids, tended to the wounded children.

An hour passed.

Two.

Three.

"Blast it!" Herzlos barked. He had lost two hundred men to injury or to whatever was happening behind the wall. Absolutely zero progress had been made. "Blast it, curse it, boil it!"

He didn't actually say any of those things. He said words that I would never, ever print in a book.

Feel free to use your imagination.

The children were growing tired. But they had a burgeoning stack of unconscious men lined up along the bottom of the stockade. Occasionally, one would come to, and a kid would knock him out again with a frying pan.

The day wore on. The sun moved into the west.

Herzlos rode his black charger back and forth, back and forth before his men, cursing and scowling. And then, as the sun began to dip in the orange sky, Herzlos looked up at Jorinda and Joringel on the top of the wall at exactly the same moment as they looked down at him.

Their eyes locked.

The children smiled.

"That's it!" Herzlos exploded. "Forget them all!" (He didn't say "Forget them all.") "All of them! Bring forth the machines of war!"

The call was repeated back along the lines of soldiers. "BRING FORTH THE MACHINES OF WAR!"

"BRING FORTH THE MACHINES OF WAR!"

"BRING FORTH THE MACHINES OF WAR!"

Joringel frowned. "What are machines of war?"

Jorinda's face had gone ashen. She gazed out over the armies and murmured, "You don't want to know."

ADAM GIDWITZ

The ladders were withdrawn from the wall. The soldiers trapped inside fought with the children.

At last, the final soldier inside the wall fell. The children all heaved and panted, sweat dripping down their faces. Among them lay the unconscious forms of hundreds of soldiers. Their bodies lay in heaps upon the dry pine needles, dappled with the golden afternoon sun.

"Huzzah!" cried the little boy with the gap between his teeth. Soon the cry was taken up by all the children. "Huzzah! Huzzah! Huzzah!"

Jorinda said to Eva, "Go tell them to dump the unconscious soldiers in the ravine. With any luck, they'll come to in the middle of the night and just wander home."

"Shouldn't we keep them as hostages?" Joringel asked.

But Jorinda replied, "Herzlos doesn't care about hostages. He wants blood."

Eva slipped down the ladder to deliver Jorinda's orders. Soon, the bodies were being dragged away as Jorinda and Joringel's mother directed the care for the injured children.

The sun began to dip in the sky. Outside the walls, soldiers started to set up camp. Jorinda and Joringel watched. "They may not attack again tonight," Joringel speculated. Jorinda said nothing. She watched the horizon.

"They're coming," she said suddenly.

"What?"

Jorinda swallowed hard. "The machines of war."

"How do you know?" Joringel peered into the distance.

"Listen."

Joringel listened. Sure enough, he could just make out a faint rumbling through the trees.

"What are machines of war?"

Jorinda didn't answer. Down below, soldiers were clearing a path. Smaller trees were being cut down.

"They must be huge," Joringel murmured.

And then, from out of a close of cedar, two wooden wheels appeared, and then two more. They bore a platform. On the platform was a giant arm, with a cup at one end. In the cup was an enormous boulder.

Joringel stopped breathing. "What . . . what is it?"

Jorinda felt her fingers creep to her temples. She said, "It's called a catapult."

Rolling on four wheels, the giant wooden catapult moved into a space the archers made for it. Behind the catapult came oxcarts— one, two, three, four . . . Each one carried enormous boulders. Six men ran around the catapult, loosing ropes and checking springs.

Behind it, another catapult appeared through the trees.

And then one more.

Joringel stared at the war machines, trying to figure out what they were for. The six men who tended the first catapult were looking at the darkening sky and discussing something furiously. A captain rode his horse up to the group and dismounted. Jorinda and Joringel watched as the six men shook their heads and raised their hands.

"What's going on?" Joringel asked. Jorinda did not know. They squinted to make out the men's faces. Darkness was falling fast. Inside the fortress, the bonfire had been lit. Unconscious soldiers were being unceremoniously dumped in the ravine that ran along the side of the wood.

Outside the wall, Herzlos spurred his horse around and trotted up to his front lines. He called up to Jorinda and Joringel.

"Surrender, blast it!" he cried. "Surrender, or we'll bring this wall down!"

Jorinda didn't respond. Her fingers still worked at her temples.

"You know what these can do, girl! After all, *you* had them made!"

"You did?" Joringel hissed.

Jorinda pressed her lips together and nodded. The sky in the west was a mess of red and orange. In the east, it was nearly black. She took a deep breath. She cried, "You can't fire on us. Not tonight. It's too dark."

Herzlos squinted up at the little girl. After a moment, he glanced angrily back at his catapults, and then up to Jorinda.

Joringel whispered, "Are you bluffing?"

Jorinda's lips were white. Joringel looked back and forth from his sister to King Herzlos, who was glaring up at them through the gathering gloom.

At last, Herzlos cried, "Boil your head!" (Or something like it.) "You have until dawn to surrender! Then we unleash a rain of fiery death down upon you and your little brats. Once we begin, we will not stop. Not until every one of you is dead." He jerked his horse's head back toward his troops and rode away, framed by the crimson sunset.

Joringel gazed at the machines of war, all bristling with wooden levers and twining ropes, laden with their enormous, craggy boulders. "Can we stop them? The catapults?"

Slowly, Jorinda shook her head back and forth. "No," she said quietly. "No, we can't."

The children sat around the great bonfire, their faces solemn in the dancing light. No one could sleep. Fear of the morning—of machines of war and soldiers bent on bloodshed—pricked at the children's hearts and peeled their exhausted eyelids back from their eyes. Those who tried to lie down soon sat up in a panting sweat. Tomorrow was the day of judgment. Tomorrow, many of them would be dead.

Jorinda and Joringel's mother gazed out at the troubled faces of the children. "They need something to take their minds off the morrow," she said.

Jorinda shrugged. "So do I."

"Well?" her mother asked. "I've been trying to hold off, but I suppose now might be the time. Will you tell me where you've been? What you've done over the last year?"

Joringel's head had been buried in his arms. He looked up at his sister.

Jorinda said, "It's kind of a long story."

Eva, sitting nearby, said, "That's my favorite kind."

Joringel smiled, but shook his head. "We just told the whole thing . . ."

"To whom?" asked their mother.

Jorinda looked at Joringel. He shrugged. She smiled. "To the Devil. And his grandmother."

Their mother furrowed her brow. "What?"

Eva leaned over. "What?"

The little boy with the gap in his teeth said, "Well, now we've *got* to hear it."

Their mother said, quietly, "It might lift their morale."

Jorinda looked out over the children. They were a despondent, desultory crew.

Jorinda's and Joringel's eyes met.

Jorinda half smiled.

And Joringel said, "Okay."

He pulled himself up on the great log so he was sitting beside his sister, and the children by the fire pulled their thin blankets closer around their bodies. And Joringel began:

Once upon a time, in the days when fairy tales really happened, there lived a man and his wife . . .

"Whoa!" cried Eva. "How did your voice get like that?"

Joringel grinned and shrugged. "I don't know. It tends to do that when I tell the story."

"Weird," whispered the little boy.

Their mother squinted curiously at her son.

Joringel went on, and indeed, his voice was so bold and clear that children a hundred yards away from the bonfire, tossing and turning under ragged blankets, sat up and listened.

More than anything else—more than their house, their garden, their tree—this couple wanted a child. But they did not have one . . .

All night, Jorinda and Joringel told their story. The children gasped and laughed and stared at Jorinda and Joringel in disbelief.

Their mother bit her lip and hung on her children's every word. The moon dipped down in the west just as the sky in the east grew gray with dawn. Birds started to sing in the branches above the children's heads. The bonfire guttered and died, its rich, smoky smell wafting over the little kingdom in the trees.

When Jorinda and Joringel got to the part of the story in the Märchenwald, their mother sat straight up. When they spoke, in their booming, bold voices, of meeting a man who claimed to be narrating stories from their world, their mother scratched her head. When he talked about telling his own story, and how it helped him, she started to smile.

Jorinda and Joringel told the tale through their time in Hell. Then their mother insisted on hearing what happened next.

"But you were there for it!" Joringel objected.

"Please," his mother whispered. "I think it will help."

So they told of returning to Grimm. Of gathering the children. Of making a life out here in the woods.

"Go on," their mother urged them.

They told of the soldiers coming, and the battle that had raged through the day.

Finally, when they spoke of the machines of war rolling through the trees, their hearts began hammering in their chests, their breath grew short, and they could not go on.

At last, the clearing was silent in the gray dawn, save for the birds.

"What happens next?" their mother asked. The children of Grimm leaned forward to hear. Mist rose from the forest floor. A bullfrog croaked in the distance.

"Nothing," said Jorinda. "That's it. We told you a story. Now we're here."

"But what happens next?" their mother asked again.

Her children shrugged. "We don't know. It hasn't happened yet," said Joringel.

"The catapults fire on us, and we all die?" Jorinda muttered.

Their mother's eyes crinkled at the corners. "You're telling your story, right?" Joringel nodded. Jorinda watched the glowing embers of the bonfire. "So? Keep telling it. What happens next?"

Jorinda and Joringel glanced at each other, confused.

In the rising dawn outside the walls, soldiers rushed back and forth across the great camp. Men and women donned their mail and sharpened their weapons. The teams of soldiers operating the catapults tightened ropes and shouted orders at one another. King Herzlos rode his black charger back and forth before his assembled troops.

Finally, one of the technicians called out, "Your majesty! We're ready!"

Herzlos nodded and spurred his horse. "AT ARMS!" he cried. "AT ARMS!"

Three thousand soldiers lifted their weapons to their shoulders and advanced to their places before the wooden wall. Catapult cranks whined loudly as they were turned.

"JORINDA! JORINGEL!" Herzlos cried. "THIS IS YOUR LAST CHANCE TO SURRENDER! THE CATAPULTS AWAIT!" He was answered with silence. So he leaned his head back and bellowed, "SURRENDER, OR DIE!"

Inside the walls, the children heard Herzlos. They had not prepared for battle. They still sat on the ground, half covered in blankets, listening to Jorinda and Joringel's mother as she instructed her children to keep telling their story. A shiver of panic ran through the group.

But the twins' mother stared steadily at her children. "Just tell us what happens next."

"They're about to assault the fortress, Mama," said Joringel.

"We should be getting ready," added Jorinda, anxiety beginning to lace her voice. "We should have been getting ready hours ago."

"Tell us what happens next," their mother insisted. Her voice was firm.

"Why?" Joringel asked. The children around the campfire shifted nervously, eyes darting between Jorinda and Joringel on the one hand and their mother on the other.

"Tell us," their mother repeated. "Tell us."

Jorinda rolled her eyes. "Fine," she snapped. "Another great piece of advice from our brilliant mother." Her mother winced.

Once upon a time, Jorinda began, her voice laced with angry sarcasm, *a kingdom of children sat on the ground behind a great wall. They were scared.*

Beyond the wall was arrayed the largest army the Kingdom of Grimm had ever seen. At its head rode a tyrant bent on murdering kids. As dawn rose, that army had prepared for battle, while inside the walls, the children sat and listened to stories.

Shivers of anxiety ricocheted among the children of Grimm.

The soldiers lined up before the wooden wall, and the catapults were readied for the assault. Technicians turned huge iron cranks to tighten the coils of rope. Soldiers dressed the enormous boulders with cloth, soaked in oil. King Herzlos cried to the walls—

"SURRENDER, JORINDA! THIS IS YOUR LAST FLIPPING CHANCE." A shiver ran through the children. "JORINGEL! SURRENDER!"

Jorinda faltered for a moment. Her face grew longer, paler.

But Herzlos's cry was not answered—because the children were telling a story. So he raised his arm. Three thousand soldiers stood at attention. Three catapults strained at their great, wooden triggers. Three great boulders, covered in oiled cloth, were lit with flame. They hissed in their wooden cups. Herzlos dropped his arm. Three triggers were pulled. Three flaming boulders rose on high arcs into the sky—

Children began to scream. Joringel looked at them, and then up. Hanging in the air, tracing a high arc against the clear blue sky, were three orbs of fire—like three new suns. They seemed to move very slowly, gaining altitude. The screams of the children sounded far away. As the great fiery orbs reached the top of their parabola, they stopped and hung, just for an instant, in midair. And then they began to fall. Slowly at first. Then faster. And faster. And suddenly the screams of the children were very loud, and there was a rushing, roaring sound from the fire as it tore the air, followed by a horrific crash.

One of the stones hit the wall from directly above, shearing off the top five feet of the strong wooden structure and burying itself at the wall's base. Its flames licked the dry wood and lashed ropes. A second stone went sailing over the children's heads. It landed with a crash on the very edge of the quarry, where the trees were thin. It scattered them like ninepins, and then went caroming over the side of the cliff. The third stone landed with a sickening thud at the edge of the group of children and came to rest on a small girl's leg. She screamed horribly, and the children around her tried to yank her away from the stone and beat the flames from her clothes.

"Quickly," Jorinda and Joringel's mother said. "Keep telling the story! Now!"

Jorinda's eyes were wide, staring at the horrible scene. She stammered. Joringel cut in.

Outside the wall, soldiers cheered.

As he said it, the children heard the sound rise up from beyond the wall.

Boulders were fetched from the oxcarts that stood waiting and were heaved onto the great wooden spoons. Herzlos shouted at his troops, "Don't attack until my word! Wait until the catapults have done their job!"

Jorinda went on:

The ropes coiled back around the catapults' crankshafts. The oiled cloth on the stones was set aflame. Herzlos raised his arm. He dropped it. Three burning boulders traced their high, silent arc into the air, and—

A horrible tearing sound ripped through the wood. The

children saw the top of their great wall shorn clear off in three different places. The boulders went careening into the clearing. Children leaped to their feet and dove out of the way.

"Now what?" their mother cried. "What happens now?" Children were screaming and huddling together. Suddenly, the fire from one of the boulders caught the pine needles on the ground. Flame swept out from the rock in a great wave. The children's screams became shrill with panic.

Jorinda looked helplessly at Joringel.

"I don't know!" he cried, his voice practically drowned by the roar of the spreading fire and the screams of the children.

"*You're* telling the story!" their mother cried. "It's *your* story!"

Joringel shrugged, dumb with panic.

Jorinda grabbed her hair with her hands. Children beat at the flames on the ground and screamed as the fire spread in a great circle around them.

"You've told your story!" their mother shouted over the roar of the flames. "Now use it. Use what you know! Make something new!"

And suddenly, they understood.

Jorinda's eyes found Joringel's.

Make something new.

In the midst of the fire, and the screaming, they understood.

That tears can bear a boat upon their waters. That weeds can blossom into wildflowers. That stone can be carved into art. Joringel began:

From up in a high red cedar, three ravens stared angrily at the carnage on the forest floor.

"It isn't right," said the first raven.

Up above, in the tree, the first raven said exactly that.

"We should do something about it," said the second.

Up in the tree, the second repeated Joringel's words. Then he added, "Wait, we should?"

"I'm gonna kill them!" the third raven screamed. And as Joringel described it, the raven did scream that. He began beating his wings angrily against the air. *"I'm gonna beat in their brains, I'm gonna break their legs, I'm gonna tear off their—"*

"We get it," said the first raven.

"Well? What do we do?" said the second, hopping around the branch in agitation.

"Defend the forest!" the third raven cried. "Defend the kingdom! Defend the children!"

And with that, he dove from the branch. His two brothers, inspired by his courage, dove right after him.

Outside the wall, Herzlos grinned gleefully. The fortress was a ruin of fire and splinters. Soon his men would be able to pour

ADAM GIDWITZ

in and take the children by storm. Dead or alive. "Catapults!" he cried. "Ready your—"

Suddenly, there was an explosion of black feathers. Herzlos went staggering backward, stunned.

A large black raven was suddenly stabbing at the tyrant with his beak. Herzlos waved his arms at it frantically, trying to beat it back. His men stared at the surreal sight. They had never seen a king attacked by a bird.

Just as he seemed to be fending the crazed raven off, a second slammed, like a missile, into Herzlos's head. The tyrant went flying earthward. He lay on his back, kicking and flailing at the two insane, homicidal black birds.

"BLAST!" he cried (he wasn't saying "Blast"). "BLASTBLASTBLAST! Help ME—EEEK!" This last scream came as the third raven plunged right between Herzlos's legs, beak first. Herzlos's hands flew to his groin, while trying to cover his face with his arms. It was no good. The ravens thrashed him mercilessly.

Inside the fortress, Joringel went on:

His soldiers stared as the great, the terrifying, the merciless King Herzlos writhed on the ground, being attacked by a storm of black feathers and sharp black beaks. Herzlos screamed and screamed and screamed.

Jorinda grinned and took over.

Still, the soldiers had their orders. As the catapults were loaded with great, flaming stones, the men readied their swords and spears and shields, steadying themselves for the final assault on the fortress of children. But before the crankshafts were set, before the men could rush the broken wall, a strange sound came echoing through the wood.

It sounded like howling and roaring and baying and barking and growling all at once. As if some horrible menagerie of beasts was about to be unleashed on the soldiers from behind. The men at the back turned to look. And indeed, they saw one of the strangest sights they had ever beheld.

Joringel knew what was coming. He bit his lip and smiled. Jorinda continued:

They saw a monster of a man: enormous, hideous, his huge body terminating at the top of his shoulders—which towered over a long scrawny neck, craning out like a vulture's. A bald head with a great white beard, tiny black teeth, and round, red-rimmed eyes was perched at the end of the neck. This ogre held a dozen chains, and at the end of each, a black beast, huge and ferocious and slavering, bayed and cried and struggled to be set loose.

And indeed the children could, from over the wall, hear a cacophony of wild animal noises.

The soldiers who saw the beasts dropped their weapons

ADAM GIDWITZ

and fled. The great ogre Malchizedek loosed the animals from their chains. The beasts flew at the undefended flank of Herzlos's army. A great black cat landed on one soldier and broke his spine with a swipe of his claws. A dog the size of a wolf grabbed another soldier by the thigh and tore his leg clean off. A great black bear cuffed a man so hard his head crumpled in his helmet. Soldiers screamed and ran. And then Malchizedek himself pulled a great, double-headed battle-ax from his back and began swinging it. Terror swept the left flank of Herzlos's army.

Just then, the children saw some soldiers crawling over the holes in the great wall. One man had made it over and was coming right for the children. Some of the bigger kids rushed to greet him. But the soldier, seeing them, screamed, turned to one side, and kept running. He had not been coming for them. No. He was running for his life.

Still, Joringel went on, *the right flank of Herzlos's army pressed forward, ready to assault the remains of the fortress. Three captains beat at the ravens, trying to rescue their king. "Forget me!" Herzlos cried. "Fire the catapults! Fire the catapults and assault the flipping fortress! NOW!" A raven poked him in the eye. "BLAST!"*

Inside the fortress, the fire had spread. There was now a towering wall of it, running from one end of the clearing to another. It ate up the ground and licked at the frightened children.

"Hurry!" Jorinda and Joringel's mother cried. "Finish this!"

Jorinda gazed at the carnage. Joringel shook his head. "How?"

"I don't know." Jorinda's face was pale.

The children near them stared desperately.

And then Joringel said, "Eddie?"

The panic slid from Jorinda's face. She said, "Eddie."

Jorinda was suddenly speaking as quickly as she could, letting her voice boom out over the screams of the children and roar of the fire.

The earth began to shake.

And indeed, the earth began to shake.

Children were thrown from their feet.

Children were, in fact, thrown from their feet.

And then there was a peal like thunder. It was so loud that everyone—children inside the wall, soldiers outside of it—bent over and grabbed their ears.

All of that happened.

Then came the sound of tearing and scraping and ripping, as if stone was being rent asunder.

Which, Joringel cut in, *it was. For up out of the granite quarry that lay behind the clearing, erupting from beneath the stone, there rose an enormous creature. His skin was pink, but thin—so thin you could see his black bones through it.*

As he said this, a giant, fleshy mass appeared.

It rose from behind the cliff. It was a wide, pink head, and then a black spine, a huge, pink belly, and finally a great, massive, fleshy tail.

Jorinda and Joringel were gaping and grinning at the same time. For as Joringel described it, the creature did indeed rise out of the quarry. The children said, in unison,

It was the Eidechse von Feuer, der Menschenfleischfressende.

And they pronounced it perfectly.

And then the gigantic body came crashing down in the clearing, and children were thrown this way and that, and the creature roared—so loud and long it blew the trees backward and knocked half the wall down. The soldiers suddenly could see into the clearing. They did not like what they saw.

They saw a humongous beast—a humongous pink salamander—roaring and blowing fire from its mouth into the sky.

Then it stopped.

There was a moment of total silence, when not a soldier, not a child, not a single leaf moved, as if all were paralyzed by the deafening sound, the horrible sight, and the vomitous smell of the giant beast.

A raven landed next to Jorinda. "Eddie says hi."

And then three catapults loosed three flaming boulders into the air.

They traced a tall arc. At their zenith, each paused, high, high above the earth, their flaming orange framed by the blue sky. Then they fell. Right for the huddled, frightened children.

Joringel bared his teeth and said,

The Eidechse von Feuer, der Menschenfleischfressende, watched the great boulders as they screamed toward the ground. He bounded to his left and wrapped his huge, fleshy body around a thousand screaming children.

A thousand screaming children were suddenly enveloped in Eddie's pink, foul-smelling flesh.

The fiery boulder crashed to the earth, igniting the pine needles all around the children, and then went rolling past them and off the side of the cliff. The flames raged all around the clearing. The air was so thick with smoke and heat it was getting hard to breathe. Eddie stayed wrapped around the children as the flames licked his skin.

Everything happened just as Joringel was describing it. Jorinda took over:

A second boulder, its aim perfect and deadly, fell exactly where Jorinda and Joringel had been standing a moment ago. But now, the Eidechse von Feuer, der Menschenfleischfressende, stood there, with Jorinda and Joringel and all the other children huddled behind him.

Suddenly, a boulder slammed into Eddie's side. The children ducked their heads. Eddie was rocked sideways. The boulder exploded on impact. Eddie began to make a sound like hacking, or coughing.

"Is he hurt?" Jorinda cried.

A raven, huddling for protection between Jorinda's legs, said, "No! That's him laughing."

"Really?"

"Really!"

Joringel went on.

And then a third boulder completed its arc. This one was aimed deeper. Directly for the center of the children. Their screams became shrill. The flaming stone would not hit Eddie. It would fly over him. It would land on top of hundreds of children—

And just as the third boulder plummeted into the cowering crowd, Eddie flicked his enormous fleshy tail over their heads and smacked the boulder with it. And the stone exploded. Like fireworks. Like the largest display of fireworks you've ever seen. A million microscopic shards of flame flew all over the forest, and the children gaped at the most beautiful display of pyrotechnics ever witnessed in the Storied Kingdoms.

The Eidechse von Feuer, der Menschenfleischfressende,

lifted his head and opened his mouth and sprayed a column of fire, red and white and aquamarine, looping across the clearing and over the remains of the wall. The kids who had not done so already threw themselves to the ground, and for an instant it was as if they were all lying beneath one giant quilt of flame.

When it finally subsided, Jorinda said:

The Eidechse von Feuer, der Menschenfleischfressende, leaped forward, smothering the flames that raced over the clearing.

Which Eddie instantly did, extinguishing the flames with his great, pink body.

He blew another column of flame over the heads of Herzlos's soldiers. They screamed like babies.

The soldiers duly screamed like babies.

He advanced upon them, shattering the wall under his huge frame, roaring and blowing fire into the sky. The soldiers leaped to their feet and ran for their stinking lives.

All of that happened. Joringel grinned at his sister. She looked like she was having fun. He took over.

As Eddie approached, Herzlos the oppressor cowered on the ground, unable to rise from where the ravens had beaten him. When the great salamander opened his leviathan jaws again, every remaining soldier ran—save Herzlos. And when

Eddie blew his fire across the forest floor, Herzlos glowed like a red ember, and then grayed, and then blackened. And died.

It happened just as Joringel described it.

The rest of the soldiers fled, and the great salamander went loping after them, roaring and blowing fire to the heavens. The children cheered. Malchizedek wiped his brow and smiled. His creatures padded up to him, rubbing their glossy, obsidian coats against one another. And the three ravens pumped their wings and chest-bumped and spun in manic, delirious circles.

Jorinda and Joringel silently watched the celebrations. And then Jorinda reached out her little hand, and Joringel reached out his, and they held on to one another.

And then their mother came up behind them and put her arms around their small, heaving shoulders, and held on to them, too.

And as Jorinda and Joringel watched the giant pink salamander chasing Herzlos's armies, and the children celebrating, and an ogre grinning, and three ravens dancing around like idiots, they at last understood that their problems would never have been solved by trying to cover them up or choke them back or pretend they didn't exist. By repression.

No, their problems could only be solved by expression. By telling their tales, and by making up new ones, too.

And if you don't know what I'm talking about, that's okay. I do.

Now that I've said it, I do.

And now, after three novels, hundreds of pages, and more death and despair than should ever be printed in books ostensibly written for children, we have finally arrived at

The End

Almost. One more thing.

There is a new kingdom now, nestled in the high red trees by the edge of the quarry. It is called the Jungreich—the Kingdom of Children.

That's pronounced YOONG-RIKE. In case you were wondering.

There is no king, no queen in the Jungreich. Children are allowed to live their lives there—to run, to play, to tell their tales. At night, they go home to their parents in the Kingdom of Grimm. Mostly. And they go to school and do their chores. Mostly. But they venture into the woods whenever they want to—to tell their tales and face their fears and let whatever is inside out.

Back in the Castle Grimm, the prince has been restored to the throne. He is not very clever, but he has grown rather kind. And he employs Jorinda and Joringel's mother as his most trusted adviser. So he rules fairly and well. His marriage to Jorinda, of course, has been annulled.

Jorinda and Joringel live with their mother in the castle. She loves them deeply, manifestly, devotedly—just as she always meant to.

And they will all live happily ever after.

The End

Wait! I forgot! One last thing!

Every once in a while, Jorinda and Joringel venture back into the Märchenwald. They come to see me.

And also Hansel and Gretel.

And Jack and Jill.

Yeah, I know them, too.

And I order pizza, and we all sit and tell each other stories until the sidewalks are empty, and the sirens stop their wailing, and the sun rises over the bleary streets of Brooklyn.

Which is, of course, how I learned all these tales to begin with.

And now it really is,

The End

Probably.

Where Do These Stories Come From?

You should have your own beloved book of Grimm—a tome that you turn to in search of humor, solace, and nightmares. I have mine. It's a large, red, tattered, cloth-covered volume, translated by Ralph Manheim. I love Manheim's style: lyrical simplicity, I'd call it. I have thrice quoted him verbatim in these pages: in the passage describing the mother's pregnancy (on pages 4–5) and when Briar Rose's castle falls asleep and then awakens (pages 117 and 127).

The chapter *Jorinda and Joringel* has nothing in common with the Grimm tale "Jorinda and Joringel" save the names of its protagonists and the love they feel for one another. While I like the Grimm tale a lot, I chose not to retell it. I did choose, though, to steal those two names. I mean, Jorinda and Joringel? How could I not?

The chapters *Jorinda and Joringel* and *The Juniper Tree* are really two halves of the Grimm tale "The Juniper Tree." My favorite version of that tale is the translation by Lore Segal, illustrated by the incomparable Maurice Sendak.

The chapter *Ashputtle* is a near verbatim transcription of my retelling of Grimm's "Ashputtle." If you've ever heard me speak to children, you've likely heard the exact words from the chapter, delivered amid a torrent of children screaming. The passage about chamber pots and ashes and cinders was suggested by Laura Amy Schlitz; while I haven't followed up this particular point with proper research, it is far too good to omit.

The Three Hanging Men and *Malchizedek's Mansion* are two halves of the same Grimm tale, "The Boy Who Left Home to Find Fear." I came across the name Malchizedek when visiting a medieval church. Melchizedek [I changed the spelling] is a priest mentioned in the Bible. There was a picture of him on the walls. He looked kind of scary. Also, like Jorinda and Joringel, his name was too awesome not to steal.

The chapter *Sleeping Beauty* was inspired by the Grimm tale "Briar Rose." While the ridiculous golden plates scenario is absolutely original, I changed her affliction as well as the resolution of the story. That she is woken by a chunk of apple being dislodged from her throat, instead of being kissed, comes from the Grimm version of "Snow White." Also kissing is gross.

The Little Foal is inspired not by any Grimm tale, but instead by a story from Peter Dickinson's book *Merlin Dreams*. *Merlin Dreams* is currently, cruelly, out of print. I hope someone rectifies this, as it is one of my very favorite collections of stories.

The Ivory Monkey (and its reprise in Hell) was inspired by Eric A. Kimmel's retelling *Anansi and the Moss-Covered Rock*. Before any of my work was published, and having attempted my very first adaptation of a Grimm story, I wrote to Mr. Kimmel and asked him for advice. He gave me both advice and encouragement. It is amazing when your literary heroes turn out to be heroes in real life, too.

The stack of mattresses that serves as a theme throughout, and is realized in the chapter *The Tyrants*, was suggested by the Hans Christian Andersen story "The Princess and the Pea."

The remaining chapters are based on sawdust and spit and experience. Sammy and George and Jeff were actual students of mine, but they never did anything quite as bad as I describe in this book. Except for Jeff, who really did glue cotton balls to his face.

Sometimes people ask me why dark fairy tales have enjoyed such a renaissance of late. I think the reason is this:

Most fairy tales have roughly the same structure. A hero faces a problem at home—she's poor, he's the neglected youngest son, their parents are trying to murder them, etc. The hero leaves home and ventures into a strange world—often a forest. In the forest, the hero faces dangers and difficulties—weird, frightening, and grim—and ultimately overcomes them. Finally, the hero returns home, stronger, richer, and wiser.

Being the reader of a dark fairy tale is much like being the hero of one. Our lives are filled with pain, boredom, and fear. We want to venture into the dark wood, to see the oddities and the beauties it holds, and to test ourselves against them. So we pick up a book of fairy tales. The real ones. The weird ones. The dark ones. We see oddities and beauties galore. We test our courage and our understanding. Finally, we put the book down and return to our lives. And hopefully, just like the hero of the fairy tale, we return stronger, richer, and wiser.

In difficult times—of recession and violence and political bitterness—we long for a dark forest to which we can escape; and from which we can return, better than we were before.

Acknowledgments

I would like to thank my mother and father for teaching me how to write.

My mother taught me to write in the fifth, sixth, and seventh grades. Rather than allowing me to type my own essays, she would insist on taking dictation from me, freely editing my words and ideas as I spoke. I learned a great deal about quality and content and rhetoric from these sessions. And of course, my essays during this period were brilliant, because my mother has a PhD.

My father's instruction began in eighth grade. I would write an essay, bring it to my father, and then I would run back to my room and shut the door and pray. Then I would hear, "ADAM!" I would slink down to my parents' room, where my father was sitting in a great big chair and staring at the essay. I would stand before him, and—every time, without fail—he would intone, "Tell me what you were *trying* to say." It was usually at this point that I began to cry. Because I knew that the next three to six hours would be devoted to writing and rewriting and rewriting again.

If it weren't for these experiences with my father, I know I would not be a writer today, because my editor, the brilliant Julie Strauss-Gabel, has standards even higher than my father's.

Yes, she makes me cry sometimes. But I love her for it. And my readers should, too.

My little brother did not teach me how to write. He taught me just about everything else of importance, though. The relationship between Jorinda and Joringel is drawn, in no small part, from ours.

Sarah Burnes, my agent, found me in a first-grade classroom and changed my life, like some Wise Woman from a fairy tale. I will never be able to thank her enough.

The team at Penguin has also been utterly magical. As has my assistant, Vanessa DeJesus.

And Lauren Mancia, my wife, reads my books before they are books, when they are malformed and protean and nonsensical. And she is honest with me about how malformed and protean and nonsensical they are. Which I don't really like. But she also laughs out loud at the jokes in my books. And for that I am eternally, profoundly grateful. For that and for everything.

TURN THE PAGE FOR A TEASER
FROM THE BOOK THAT
STARTED IT ALL . . .

. . . IF YOU DARE.

*O*nce upon a time, in a kingdom called Grimm, an old king lay on his deathbed. He was Hansel and Gretel's grandfather—but he didn't know that, for neither Hansel nor Gretel had been born yet.

Now hold on a minute.

I know what you're thinking.

I am well aware that nobody wants to hear a story that happens *before* the main characters show up. Stories like that are boring, because they all end exactly the same way. With the main characters showing up.

But don't worry. This story is like no story you've ever heard.

You see, Hansel and Gretel don't just *show up* at the end of this story.

They show up.

And then they get their heads cut off.

Just thought you'd like to know.

The old king knew he was soon to pass from this world, and so he called for his oldest and most faithful servant. The servant's name was Johannes; but he had served the king's father, and his father's father, and his father's father's father so loyally that all called him Faithful Johannes.

Johannes tottered in on bowed legs, heaving his crooked back step by step and leering with his one good eye. His long nose sniffed at the air. His mouth puckered around two rotten teeth. But, despite his grotesque appearance, when he came within view, the old king smiled and said, "Ah, Johannes!" and drew him near.

The king's voice was weak as he said, "I am soon to die. But before I go, you must promise me two things. First, promise that you will be as faithful to my young son as you have been to me."

Without hesitation, Johannes promised.

The old king went on. "Second, promise that you will show him his entire inheritance—the castle, the treasures, all this fine land—*except* for one room. Do not show him the room with the portrait of the golden princess. For if he sees the portrait he will fall madly in love with her. And I fear it will cost him his life."

The king gripped Johannes's hand. "Promise me."

Again Johannes promised. Then the wrinkles of worry left the king's brow, and he closed his eyes and breathed his last.

Soon the prince was crowned as the new king. He was celebrated with parades and toasts and feasts all throughout the kingdom. But, when the revelry finally abated, Johannes sat him down for a talk.

First, Johannes described to him all of the responsibilities of the throne. The young king tried not to fall asleep.

Then he explained that the old king had asked him to show the young king his entire inheritance—the castle, the treasures, all this fine land. At the word *treasures* the young king's face lit up. Not that he was greedy. It was just that he found the idea of treasures exciting.

Finally, Johannes tried to explain his own role to the young king. "I have served your father, and your father's father, and your father's father's father before that," Johannes said. The young king started calculating on his fingers how that was even possible, but before he could get very far, Johannes had moved on. "They call me Faithful Johannes because I have devoted my life to the Kings of Grimm. To helping them. To advising them. To under-standing them."

"Understanding them?" the young king asked.

"No. Under-standing them. In the ancient sense of the word. Standing beneath them. Supporting them. Bearing their troubles and their pains on my shoulders."

The young king thought about this. "So you will under-stand me, too?" he asked.

"I will."

"No matter what?"

"Under any circumstances. That is what being faithful means."

"Well, under-stand that I am tired of this, and would like to see the treasures now." And the young king stood up.

Faithful Johannes shook his head and sighed.

They began by exploring every inch of the castle—the treasure crypts, the towers, and every single room. Every single room, that is, save one. One room remained locked, no matter how many times they passed it.

Well, the young king was no fool. He noticed this. And so he asked, "Why is it, Johannes, that you show me every room in the palace, but never *this* room?"

Johannes squinted his one good eye and curled up his puckered, two-toothed mouth. Then he said, "Your father asked me not to show you that room, Your Highness. He feared it might cost you your life."

I'm sorry, I need to stop for a moment. I don't know what you're thinking right now, but when I first heard this part of the story, I thought, "What, is he crazy?"

Maybe you know something about young people, and maybe you don't. I, having been one myself once upon a time, know a few things about them. One thing I know is that if you don't want one to do something—for example, go into a room where there's a portrait of an unbearably beautiful princess—saying "It might cost you your life" is about the *worst* thing you could possibly say. Because then that's *all* that young person will want to do.

I mean, why didn't Johannes say something else? Like, "It's a broom closet. Why? You want to see a broom closet?" Or, "It's a fake door, silly. For decoration." Or even, "It's the ladies' bathroom, Your Majesty. Best not go poking your head in there."

Any of those would have been perfectly sufficient, as far as I can tell.

But he didn't say any of those things. If he had, none of the horrible, bloody events to follow would ever have happened.

(Well, in that case, I guess I'm glad he told the truth.)

"Cost me my life?!" the young king proclaimed with a toss of his head. "Nonsense!" He insisted he be let into the room. First he demanded. But Johannes refused. Then he commanded. Still Johannes refused. Then he threw himself on the floor and had a fit, which was very unbecoming for a young man the king's age. Finally, Faithful Johannes realized there was little he could do. So, wrinkling his old, malformed face into a wince, he unlocked and opened the door.

The king burst into the room. He found himself staring, face-to-face with the most beautiful portrait of the most beautiful woman he had ever seen in his life. Her hair looked like it was spun from pure gold thread. Her eyes flashed like the ocean on a sunny day. And yet, around her lips, there was a hint of sadness, of loneliness.

The young king took one look at her and fainted dead away.

———

ADAM GIDWITZ

Later, in his room, he came to. Johannes hovered over his bed. "Who was that radiant creature?" the king asked.

"That, Your Majesty, is the golden princess," Johannes answered.

"She's the most beautiful woman in the world," the young king said.

And Johannes answered, "Yes, she is."

"And yet she looked almost sad. Why is that?"

Johannes took a deep breath, and replied, "Because, young king, she is cursed. Every time she has tried to marry, her husband has died; and it is said that a fate worse than death is destined for her children, if ever she should have any. She lives in a black marble palace, topped with a golden roof, all by herself. And, as you can imagine, she is terribly lonely and terribly sad."

The king sat straight up in his bed and grabbed the front of Faithful Johannes's tunic. And though he stared into the old man's face, he saw only the princess's ocean-bright eyes and her lips ringed with sadness. "I must have her," he said. "I will marry her. I will save her."

"You may not survive," Johannes said.

"I will survive, if you help me. If you are faithful to me, if you under-stand me, you'll do it."

Johannes feared for the young king's life. But he had understood the young king's father, and his father's father, and his father's father's father before that. What could he say?

Johannes sighed. "I'll do it."

It was widely known that in all the golden princess's days of loneliness, the only thing that gave her any modicum of happiness was gold. So Johannes told the king to gather all of the gold in the kingdom and to command his goldsmiths to craft the most exquisite golden objects that the world had ever seen. Which soon was done.

Then Johannes disguised himself and the king as merchants and loaded a ship with the golden goods. And they set off for the land of the golden princess.

As their ship's prow split the sea, Johannes tutored the king in his part: "You're a gold merchant, Your Majesty. The princess has always loved gold, but these days, it is the only thing that gives her any joy. So when I bring her to the ship, charm her not only with your gentle manners and fine looks, but also with the gold. Then, perhaps, she will be yours."

When they landed, the king readied the ship and tended to his merchant costume, while Johannes, carrying a few golden objects in his bag, made his way to the towering ramparts of black marble where the golden princess lived. He entered the courtyard, and there discovered a serving girl retrieving water from a well with a golden bucket.

"Pretty maid," he said, smiling his kind but unhandsome smile, "do you think your lady might be interested in such trifling works of gold as these?" And he produced two of the finest, most exquisite golden statuettes that man's hand has ever made.

The girl was stunned by their beauty. She took them from Johannes and hurried within. Not ten minutes had elapsed before the golden princess herself emerged from the castle, holding the statuettes in her hands. She was as gorgeous as her portrait—more so in fact—and as she greeted Johannes, her golden hair flashed in the light and her ocean-blue eyes danced with pleasure. Still, around her lips there was sadness.

"Tell me, old man," she said, "are these really for sale? I've never seen anything so beautiful, so fine."

Faithful Johannes bowed. "But there is more, fair princess, much more. My master's ship is full of such wonders. And they can be yours, if you will just accompany me down to the harbor."

The princess hesitated for a moment—since her last husband-to-be had died, she had not set foot outside the palace. But the allure of the gold was too strong. She threw a shining traveling cloak over her shoulders and followed Johannes to the boat.

The young king, in his disguise as a merchant, greeted her.

Her beauty was so stunning, her sadness so apparent and so tender, that he nearly fainted again. But somehow he did not, and she smiled at him and invited him to show her all the treasures he had brought to her fair land.

As soon as they had descended below the deck, Johannes hurried to the captain of the ship, and, in whispered tones, instructed him to cast off from shore and set sail for home immediately.

Now, my young readers, I know just what you're thinking. You're thinking, *Hmmm. Stealing a girl. That's an* interesting *way of winning her heart.* Allow me to warn you now that, under any other circumstances, stealing a girl is about the worst way of winning her heart you could possibly cook up.

But, because this happened long ago, in a faraway land, it seems to have worked.

For the golden princess came back up to the deck and saw that her land was far away from her. At first she did indeed protest, and fiercely, too, that she'd been carried away by lowborn merchants. But when one of the "merchants" revealed himself to be a king, and revealed that, in addition, he was madly in love with her, and when, besides, Johannes assured her that, if she *really* wanted to, she could go home, but she couldn't take the gold if she did, the princess realized that in fact the young king was just the kind of man she would like to marry after all, and decided that she'd give the whole matrimony thing one last shot.

And they all lived happily ever after.

The End

IF YOU DARE,

join Jack and Jill as they embark on a spellbinding quest through a new set of tales from the Brothers Grimm, Hans Christian Andersen, and others. They will meet murderous mermaids, giants, goblins, and lizards made of fire.

Oh, and a frog. A talking frog.

Discover Adam Gidwitz's
acclaimed Newbery Honor Winner,

The Inquisitor's Tale

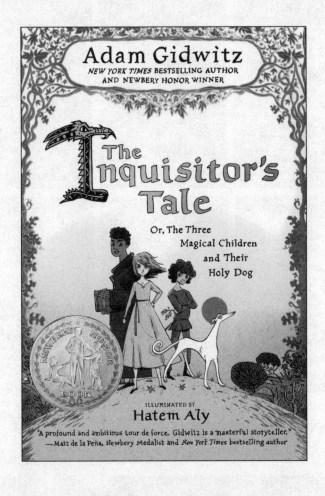

Join the adventures of
THE UNICORN RESCUE SOCIETY